I0538782

CARLOS

The Gates – Book 6

M. Tasia

ALSO BY M. TASIA

The Boys of Brighton series
Gabe
Sam's Soldiers
Rick's Bear
Jesse
Coop
Travis
Grady
Vincent
Shadow
The Holidays

The Gates series
Saint
Finn
James
Joey
Bradley

EVERYONE LOVES THE BOYS OF BRIGHTON

"I loved this book and I love this town. I hope there's going to be more."
—Melissa Lemons on *Gabe*

"An amazing read that was filled with lust, love, crazy hot sex, danger, action and so much more This is the first book I have read in this series but I will definitely be reading more in the future."
—Gay Book Reviews on *Sam's Soldiers*

"I was crazy impressed that the author made me teary over the ending of a relationship that I shouldn't have even been invested in. I didn't yet know these characters yet the author made me hurt for them. That takes some mad writing skills!"
—Love Bytes Reviews

"Jesse and Royce together have my heart. Jesse has it all by himself."
—The Book Junkie Reads on *Jesse*

"So much action, intrigue, drama and angst for the long awaited story of Grady and Ben. This was worth the wait. Sexy and sweet. I can't wait for the next."
—SamD on *Grady*

"I knew this one would be my favorite to date! There was something about Vincent that said awesome then came Tristan."
—Booky on *Vincent*

"This installment of the Boys of Brighton was so good! I loved Shadow and Randy 's story I was hooked from the first page to the last. This book was definitely worth the wait!"
—AG on *Shadow*

"I have loved this series from the very first story and this holiday novella is simply perfect. We get a glimpse of all our couples and what is happening in their lives while the holidays explode around them. I cannot wait for more!"
—bookobsessed on *The Holidays*

EVERYONE'S NEWEST LOVE – THE GATES

"Having read the entire Boys of Brighton series, I was eagerly awaiting Saint's story and it was so worth the wait. I enjoyed every word. I am always amazed by authors that bring characters to life so much that you can hardly wait for the next story. Cannot wait for Finn and Miguel to have their turn. While I'm waiting I'll reread the Boys of Brighton series!"
—Debbie Kay on *Saint*

"Ms. Tasia has done it again! This is Saint's story, for readers of the Brighton Boys, you'll know he needs a break! After being forced to become a plastic surgeon by his father, he rebels by assisting people in 3rd world countries, which puts him in the position to be kidnapped and tortured. You really feel for him, that's for sure! Max is the perfect man for poor Saint's battered soul, not that he doesn't have his own issues! Overall, this was engaging, steady paced and chock full of all the feels!"
—Avid Reader on *Saint*

"Finn and Miguel stole my heart. This is a great Sunday afternoon read. Finn's character jumped off the page as his story developed through each chapter. I loved reading his truth and watching him and Miguel find their home in each other."
—K.A. Brown on *Finn*

"Another tale from the Gates of Heaven, another two brilliant MCs we get to know very well. I loved both the plot and the characters, all their emotions and insecurities on full display. All the descriptions and world building were very vivid, providing a great background for an emotional story of self discovery and developing attraction."
—AL on *Finn*

"James...what can I say. I couldn't put it down. This is my first book in the series, so it definitely can be read and enjoyed as a standalone, but it will not be my last. Now I'm going to read the previous stories. Solid writing with a gripping style, characters that are right up my alley, and the kind of chemistry I love in my romances. What more do you need for a great reading experience."

—cinnamon on *James*

"This is really a great series and I def recommend it. I loved James and Ross, it was a rough start for the two, but they worked it out. I can't wait for more, love everything M. TASIA writes!"
—TammyKay on *James*

"I may have my new favorite book couple of the series. Joey and Sam just have that something special. At one point I was ugly crying but it was a good ugly cry if that makes any sense. I really love the series and I can't wait for her next installment!!"
—Vine Voice on *Joey*

"M. Tasia is an automatic 1 click author for me...she definitely didn't disappoint with Joey."
—Heather Weissman on *Joey*

"This author is really talented and I love her series, this one and the Boys of Brighton. Her characters are so well drawn and I can really get into the stories. I especially loved Eric in this particular book. I'm hoping Clay the rookie will be the next book. Keep 'em coming!"
—Rosemary on *Bradley*

"All the stories in this series have their own brand of excitement, this being no exception. All previous books include former heroes from the series which I find very charming. Our heroes here, Eric and Brad, give us another great performance. A villain surfaces and wreaks havoc on the lives of good people and is, after a stretch, put in his place. The book is a love story with a dose of excitement and, unfortunately, a bit of homophobia thrown in. A story nicely told."
—Tappy on *Bradley*

www.BOROUGHSPUBLISHINGGROUP.com

PUBLISHER'S NOTE: This is a work of fiction. Names, characters, places and incidents either are the product of the author's imagination or are used fictitiously. Any resemblance to actual events, locales, business establishments or persons, living or dead, is coincidental. Boroughs Publishing Group does not have any control over and does not assume responsibility for author or third-party websites, blogs or critiques or their content.

CARLOS
Copyright © 2020 M. Tasia

All rights reserved. Unless specifically noted, no part of this publication may be reproduced, scanned, stored in a retrieval system or transmitted in any form or by any means, electronic, mechanical, photocopying, recording, or otherwise, known or hereinafter invented, without the express written permission of Boroughs Publishing Group. The scanning, uploading and distribution of this book via the Internet or by any other means without the permission of Boroughs Publishing Group is illegal and punishable by law. Participation in the piracy of copyrighted materials violates the author's rights.

ISBN: 978-1-953810-09-0

This has been possible because of the love and support of my family. Love you Craig, Samantha, Katie, and Jason.

ACKNOWLEDGMENTS

Thank you to my amazing publisher for taking the time to play tour guide in her diverse and stunning area of Southern California. Your indomitable spirit and strength inspires me to continue to grow as an author. Also, to my sisters-in-law, thank you for coming along and supporting my dream. The love and strength of family is the cornerstone of my career.

CARLOS

Chapter One

Clay watched as the two men kissed, and the guests cheered for the grooms and their new life together. Miguel, typically the stoic, tough-guy type, had tears running down his face. His husband, Finn, handed him tissues. It was heartwarming to watch. Too bad Clay didn't have a soul filled with romantic dreams. He hadn't in many years.

Since being transferred to the LAPD Central Community Police Station, he felt more at ease about himself and his colleagues. His prior station in the Valley was toxic, but that was a story for another time. He wiped the memories of his homophobic brethren from his mind. He was at a wedding and was expected to be cheerful. It went against the grain, but he made an effort for his friends.

"You even going to pretend you're having a good time?" A gruff voice said from behind him.

When Clay turned to face whoever it was that felt the need to intrude on his solitude, eye level presented a broad chest with a guy so tall it forced him to look up. He was considered taller than most, but this guy was King Kong tall. "I am having a good time," he replied. "Not into all the romantic stuff though."

"Says a man staring longingly at the couple when they were saying their vows."

The guy had some pair on him. Clay should've walked away, but for some reason he didn't. "Who are you and why are we talking about me?" he asked, though he didn't care what the answer was. He preferred to be left alone. No explanations needed.

"Yeah. Okay. Carlos Fernandez. I'm Miguel's older brother." The big guy held out his hand, which engulfed Clay's. He had to be a pro wrestler or in some sort of military service like his brother, who was still on the government's payroll, but in a civilian capacity.

"Hey. I'm Clay Everett." He figured he'd be sociable. "I work with Sam, Eric, and Ross."

"Nice to meet you," Carlos replied. When he smiled, his entire face lit up, but when Carlos turned his head, Clay could make out a thin scar wrapping around his neck. "Now, back to you and your longing."

"Excuse me?"

"The look you were giving the grooms earlier," Carlos said by way of reminder.

"Okay, let's try this again. Why are we talking about this?"

"Because you looked lonely."

"You trying to hit on me?"

"No, but thanks for the offer—"

"Offer?" Clay almost choked on his beer.

"Well, if you ever need to talk or anything, you can find me at the Gates," Carlos said before walking away and joining the grooms over by the wedding cake.

What the hell just happened? One minute Clay was standing there minding his own, and then some giant comes along saying shit about him being lonely and full of longing. What the actual fuck?

"I see you've met Carlos," Alejandra, Max's mom said as she came to stand beside him. Max Connor was Miguel's boss, but it was more like Miguel was Max's right-hand man in Connor's Construction. They were doing the work restoring the Gates for Saint, the owner. Max being Saint's boyfriend came in handy. It'd gotten kind of all mixed together over there—Finn, the other groom, is the manager of the Gates restaurant, bars, and lounge areas.

"Hello ma'am," Clay said. "Yes, I've met him."

Alejandra took a seat at a nearby table and motioned for Clay to join her. He tried not to be rude to random civilians, so he sat where she had motioned for him to while taking another pull on his beer. Clay's night was getting too touchy-feely. It wasn't that she wasn't nice to talk to, but since he'd moved here five months ago, the woman had made it her mission to fix him up.

He still wasn't sure how that happened. Clay had been invited to Max's family farm in Temecula for a barbeque, and from the moment Alex, as she liked to be called, and Evie, Max's grandmother, laid eyes on him they'd been determined to set him up. He didn't think he gave off a desperate-for-a-man vibe.

"So, what do you think of him?" she asked.

"I think he's nosey, and if I told him so, he'd pile-drive me into the ground," he said.

"You're right. You need to stay away from that man," Alex advised in a grim tone.

That was a switch. "Why?" Usually, she'd be planning their wedding by now.

"Trust me, he's not ready for you," she said while pointing out a few other single attendees. "Now, that one over there, he's a doctor."

"How do you know if either of them is gay?" That could be a sticking point.

"Carlos is, but the doctor, who knows," she said with a wave of her hand in the doctor's direction. "But he's cute."

No matter how much he tried to concentrate on what Alex was saying, Clay kept seeking out the big man in the crowd. *Damn.*

***

Carlos hunkered down in Eric's spare bedroom as the party continued outside his covered window. Laughing and talking, people having a great time, and here he was hiding inside. He pulled out his sketchbook from his ever-present messenger bag, sharpened his Staedtler Lumograph graphite pencil, and opened to the first page of his new pad. Carlos had figured the new book was a metaphor for beginning his new life in LA. Clean slate and all that shit.

The first stroke of pencil to paper was always the hardest. Starting fresh, a new drawing could lead anywhere, and with that first mark on the unmarred paper it would begin.

Carlos honestly didn't know if he wanted to begin this new life here with his brother and his friends. He'd never felt comfortable anywhere, so here seemed as good a place as any to reboot his life. Considering he'd never had a stable place to call home before, he couldn't tell if this somewhere was "home" material, but he'd made a commitment to be near his brother. Anyway, he had to stick. He'd bought a condo at the Gates.

"You okay, bro?" Miguel asked from the doorway.

"Yeah, sure. I'm good. I needed a break from the festivities." He wasn't used to dealing with more than a couple people at a time. He wasn't a happy in a crowd person.

"Me too," Miguel agreed. "Who knew a small wedding would knock me out after all the years I'd spent fighting in foreign jungles."

"It was good to see you cry. I haven't seen you do that in a long time. Since Mom and Dad's funeral." Carlos remembered every last detail of that day, down to the type of flowers surrounding the caskets. Lilies in multiple colors stood on guard around their parents. Carlos had only begun to know them from a distance while working up the nerve to introduce himself. That was the day he'd found out lilies had been his mother's favorite flower.

"At least these were happy tears," Miguel said. "Finn is everything I've ever dreamed of, and I'm fortunate he said yes to being my husband."

"True, every single word," Carlos stated. "So Finn's forgiven you then?"

"Not completely," Miguel admitted. "But enough to marry me."

"Finn loves you. He would've married you anyway. Besides, you swore to me at the time that you wouldn't discuss me with anyone. We'd made our pact years ago. My existence, even if I'm only your half-brother, was supposed to remain a secret."

"You're my brother one hundred percent, no half anything. And, yeah, I swore to keep you private until you were ready."

Carlos couldn't help but smile. He loved his brother one hundred percent as well. "I told you to let me explain the situation to him."

"I know, but you're right. He loves me, and I love him. Finn understands why you did it, but his feelings are hurt. He thought I didn't trust him enough to tell him about you and how we'd met."

"At the funeral," Carlos huffed. "Of all places. Wasn't exactly how I thought it'd happen."

"That sorta shit you see on television or read in books, but damn, it happened to us for real." Miguel shook his head. His hair was still cut high and tight even though he was no longer in the military. Carlos thought it was a testament to the saying *Once a Marine, always a Marine.*

Carlos remembered the funeral. He hadn't planned on having the day go down the way it did. Miguel, the eagle-eyed Marine, noticed Carlos standing among the mourners and made a beeline straight for him. "I'm glad you were open to the idea of having a brother."

Carlos wasn't sure how things would have gone if he'd been turned away by his brother, his blood.

"You're my family. The only direct relation I have left, and the same goes for you. We need each other, bro."

"I don't know what I would've done without the letters you'd written to me from wherever you were stationed over the years. Hell, you were what, twenty-two, and I was twenty-five," Carlos reminisced. "Kids."

"It's been a lot of years. Why'd you decide to come out of your self-imposed bubble now?" Miguel asked.

"I wasn't going to miss my little brother's wedding for the world, anonymity or not. It's time for me to rejoin the world in some way. I'm not sure how, but I will."

"Man, your works hang in galleries across the globe," Miguel said. "You receive high praise at each new showing, and your art is loved. In more ways than you know, you've been out in the world for years."

"Yeah, but all communication is through my manager. No one has ever seen me or met me."

"Are you ready to put yourself back out there considering what happened the first time around?"

"Honestly, bro, I'm not sure. I'm gonna take it one step at a time. First, I needed a place to stay."

"You have a place to stay. At the Gates's hub."

"Yeah, but I've decided I needed something more permanent if I'm going to make a real go of it. I bought one of Saint's condos on the second floor."

Miguel's face lit up, his smile bright and wide. "You've decided to stay here in DTLA with us?"

"Apparently. If I want to rejoin the world, LA seems like the right place to do it." The art scene was vibrant, but more importantly, Carlos wanted to be near his brother.

"Now that you're no longer my 'secret,' I can't wait for us to do bro things together."

"Bro things?" Carlos laughed. *This should be good.*

"Yeah, like fishing and shit," Miguel said with a huff. "Or camping."

"What? You turn into the solitary fisherman, alone with his thoughts and the water when I wasn't looking? The only thing I can see you fishing with is an AK when the fish refuse to bite. As for camping, you haven't had enough sleeping under the stars, Mr. Covert Operations?"

Miguel got a thoughtful look on his face. "That might work."

"What might work?" Shit, the last thing he wanted to do was give his crazy little brother ideas.

"The AK," he said without missing a beat. "Okay, I'll admit those two things may not be right for us, but there lots of other things."

"Yeah, there are," Carlos agreed. "I've been looking forward to doing things like that as well."

Carefully, he set his sketchbook and pencil down on the side table and stood to hug his brother. Even though he had a good foot on Miguel, they looked alike. Same black hair and blue eyes, only Carlos wore his hair longer than his brother's military cut.

"Come back out to the party when you're ready," Miguel said. "No rush."

Carlos stepped back and picked up his pad with its pure, unmarred surface. He pulled the cover shut and returned his pencil to his bag. There were some things more important than his art today. He wanted to start a life with his brother.

"I'd like to return now, with you," he said to Miguel, who looked ready to cry again. "Stop it with the tears, man. You're freaking me out." Carlos jabbed Miguel in the arm before following him down the narrow hallway and back out into the reception.

Today marked the beginning of new experiences and adventures. Whether Carlos was ready for it, he'd find out over time. He was determined to give it a go and prayed he didn't regret revealing who the real CF was.

In a couple of months, he'd know one way or the other if he'd fucked up royally.

Chapter Two

The large north-facing window located in his new guestroom couldn't have been more perfect if it had been made for him. Carlos would use the blend of natural lighting and those wonderful daylight bulbs he'd put in all his light fixtures. By far, the best to paint by. Typically, he chose 5000 watt lights for his studios. The result was clean and bright, and gave him the desired effect for his paintings. He was able to bring a touch of warmth while using vibrant and true-to-life colors.

His guestroom didn't contain any furniture conducive to overnight visitors. He'd made the room his studio. He needed his workspace to be where he lived, and outside of his brother and Finn, he didn't think there was anyone he'd allow in his home. "Guestroom" was a moniker, not a reality.

His easels were set up, his chairs in place, and his paints were stored away awaiting their time to shine on the canvas. All the other bits and bobs—solvents, sketchbooks, boards, and his camera, what he considered the basics—were set in their places. His painting style was regarded as modern-day impressionism. Carlos disagreed.

His paintings may have the characteristics of impressionism, the small, thin brush strokes, his emphasis on creating the most accurate depictions of movement and lighting over time for whatever he'd chosen as his subject, but he wasn't a *plein air* painter as so many impressionists were. They worked in the open air, in front of, or surrounded by their subjects. Carlos worked inside, preferably alone, with little noise. His subjects came from the world around him, but not IRL, instead through carefully curated photographs he took over a series of days to capture the changing sunlight and feel of the area. His anxiety about human interaction and being in the middle of noise and tumult wouldn't allow more. Though he had his demons mainly under control, they could still rear their ugly head at any time.

Even as an artist, Carlos viewed himself as odd, different from the rest, outside the boundaries of human expression. A freak, but not the good kind. He wasn't stupid. He knew what people saw when they looked at him. A giant of a man, they either assumed he was a boxer or wrestler and began sizing him up to see if they could "take him" in a fight. It seemed people wanted to shove something violent on him when violence was the foremost thing he avoided in his life. He'd had enough of that. Some viewed him as scary due to his size and scar, which only fed into his belief that he functioned best outside the strictures of society.

No one would've guessed he was an artist, not in a million years, and he had preferred to keep it that way. Or at least he used to. After years of laying low and allowing his manager to deal with the shows and the sale of his work, Carlos was considering stepping out of the shadows.

Whether it was safe or prudent for him to return, he'd find out soon enough.

He took a final look around at his new studio and couldn't contain the rush of excitement he always felt when beginning a new work. Now he had to go out to find the elusive subject for this project—a person, place or thing that would grab his attention and draw him in.

He reached for his Nikon Z6 and headed for his front door. It didn't matter that the remaining rooms of his new condo were primarily filled with boxes. The most crucial space had been created, and with his bed, a kitchen, and a bathroom he was set. Now, his desire to create bloomed again.

He took the front staircase downstairs. There was also a side entrance for the tenants if they didn't want to go through the lounge area or when the restaurant and bar areas were closed and the front doors locked. He figured he'd stop by to see his brother before he took off for the day into the brilliant Californian sunshine. The light in LA was unique. As if there was a soft filter over the sun. Not so much smog as the lingering marine layer seemed to filter out the harshness near-constant sunshine held. Even in DTLA, the layer made its way between the buildings and suffused the urban feel with a warm glow.

When he reached the first level, he went over to Joey, who was working the bar in the lounge area. As he got closer, Carlos recognized two of the men sitting at the bar. Sam, Joey's boyfriend and a cop, and Sam's partner, Clay, whom Carlos had met at the wedding. Sam and Joey owned one of the condos on the second floor too.

Carlos had no idea what drew him to speak with Clay at the wedding, but whatever it was wasn't going to happen again, so Carlos kept his head down and changed directions.

At the time, he'd known better than to approach him, but Clay's eyes had drawn Carlos in. Bright azure blue encased by long black lashes had been staring at Miguel and Finn with longing while the grooms spoke their vows.

Carlos doubted anyone else had seen the look as Clay had thrown off the whole calm and indifference vibe. But, as an artist, Carlos caught the smallest details in the world around him, including how Clay felt watching his friends get married. Carlos didn't know what he was thinking when he approached a stranger to talk about deep, buried feelings. Maybe it was the pain and emotional turmoil he'd seen in those azure depths. Maybe he identified with the feelings. Whatever the reason, it wouldn't ever happen again. He didn't want to probe emotions outside the ones he felt when he painted, and he sure as hell had no intention of pissing off a cop by being a nosy pain in the ass.

Saint would know where Miguel might be, so Carlos headed to the office. He received the usual lingering looks from patrons sitting in the lounge enjoying their power lunches or whatever people did midday. The scrutiny caused him to fold into himself even further, and he raised his hand to cover the scar on his neck, staring at the floor as he went.

I can do this. They don't matter.

His hurried knock was met with a chorus of "come in." He opened the office door and bolted inside away from prying eyes. Taking a deep breath to calm himself, he turned to find Saint, Max, and his brother hovering over drawings covering one of the four desks in the room. All three looked at him with concern.

"Is something wrong?" Miguel asked as he walked around to the front of the table. "Did something happen?"

Carlos could feel his face heating up and hated that he had no control over his physical reactions, especially when people openly stared at him. "No, everything's fine. I wanted to let you know I was leaving to take some pictures. Um, can I use the back door?"

Saint and Max moved to join Miguel and Carlos's conversation. "Why do you want to use the back door?" Yeah, as he guessed, they'd think it was an odd request since it would require someone with access to the palm-scan security system to let him out.

"There are more people out front than I expected," Carlos explained, feeling as lame as he knew he sounded. He should be strong, stand up straight and proud, even if he was head and shoulders above the rest of the population at seven-two. He knew he shouldn't shy away from people, but old habits die hard, and his habits appeared to have nine lives.

"Did someone say something derogatory?" Saint asked, going straight into protection mode. Carlos noticed that about the people at The Gates. They looked out for each other. It was strange to have people he'd met only recently want to stand up for him.

"No, no, only a few stares. Nothing bad. I've been away from social gatherings for too long. I'll get used to it again." There was no way he wanted to make a big deal about insecurities he should've gotten a handle on years ago.

Carlos wasn't a coward. He'd proven that the day he'd got his scar. But he'd been withdrawn from society for so long it would take time to regrow thick skin.

"Who was staring?" Miguel asked, looking ready to rush out and defend Carlos's honor, or some shit like that.

"I'm still the older brother," Carlos jabbed, to lighten the mood. He waved his hand the length of his body. "I'm not someone who needs protection."

"So, where are you headed to take pictures?" Max asked, thankfully changing the subject. "The beach or the hills?"

"Neither. Walking the streets of DTLA." He looked forward to exploring the urban landscape. He could take a stroll the same as everyone else.

"What could be beautiful enough to be the subject for your paintings in the center of DTLA?" Max asked. "If you need a ride anywhere, one of us can take you. Maybe you'd like to go over to Malibu, the Hollywood Hills, Santa Monica, or the San Fernando Valley. Maybe the Getty Center. We have botanical gardens."

"Thanks for the offer. I may need to take you up on that in the future. Today I'd like to wander the streets," Carlos said. "You'd be surprised at the beauty you can find around. Besides, I'm looking for real-life scenes, not delicate flowers. I've been thinking about starting a new series, more urban than garden. If anyone wants to come along, I could show you."

It wasn't because he needed someone to escort him, but the company would help keep his anxiety humming at low. Also, the sight of some strange man taking pictures of odd things like steps, graffiti, arches, walkways, and whatever else he found interesting usually caused a few questions. Maybe not so much in LA. He could be taken for a tourist. He liked the idea of blending in.

"I wish I could, bro, but I'm knees-deep in drywall on the third floor."

"Yeah, same here," Max stated. "But once we get ahead of the deliveries, we could go along in a couple of days."

"Sorry, man. I would enjoy tagging along to see how you work, but I've got a mountain of paperwork to get through before my accountant arrives," Saint said. "He threatened to raise his fee if I didn't get my ass in gear."

Carlos couldn't help but be a bit disappointed, but he knew they had jobs. Before he could tell them he understood, someone knocked on the office door.

"Come in," Saint called as he returned to the drawing on one of the desks with a side-glance at the pile of paper sitting on the other counter. One look at the frustration on Saint's face told the story that paperwork was not his strong suit.

Carlos turned and saw Sam and Clay walk in. The world stopped for a fraction of a second when he came face to face with the man he'd been trying to avoid. *Shit. Time to go.*

"Okay, I'll see you guys later," he said as he walked to the door, his sightline set firmly on the floor

"Wait, Carlos. I have an idea," Miguel called. Carlos looked up to see his brother turn to Sam and Clay. "Do either of you have plans for the next couple of hours?"

"I have an appointment with my doctor for my yearly," Sam said with a definite lack of enthusiasm.

"I'm open. Whaddaya need?" Clay asked. Carlos didn't miss that the man hadn't looked his way.

"No, it's okay. I'll be fine. I don't need a chaperone," Carlos argued desperately for a way out of this impending car crash.

"Not a chaperone, but a guide," Miguel said. "Something you might need to make sure you don't turn down the wrong street."

That got the handsome police officer's attention. "Guide? Where?" He didn't sound happy. Then again, why would he be, saddled as a babysitter for a seven-foot-tall man. As if.

"Around DTLA," Saint answered. "He needs to take a few pictures."

"Pictures," Clay said with a definite lack of interest.

"I'm fine," Carlos stated.

"Clay can help," Sam said. "You're new around here."

"Tour guide?" Clay asked as if this whole situation was as distasteful to him as it was for Carlos.

"No, for Carlos's work," Miguel explained.

"What kinda work?" Clay asked. That was Carlos's signal it was time to leave before the usual happened, and comments would fly. *Carlos, an artist? Really? Come on, seriously?*

While they debated why Clay would be interested in accompanying Carlos, he made for the open doorway. He'd exit the building out the front door since it was the closest. The last thing he needed was Clay by his side. Aside from the fact that the guy hadn't taken kindly to Carlos's observations at the wedding, no one would want to tag along while someone took photos.

He was in such a hurry to reach the front door he didn't bother to check if anyone was staring. Passing the bar, he gave Joey a wave, and moments later Carlos was out on the sidewalk in the warm California sun. Taking a deep breath, he turned right and began walking fast. He needed to get far away from the building.

Carlos went a couple of blocks before he slowed and could shake off the stress of having endured that nightmare of a conversation in the office.

"Carlos, wait up, man," Clay yelled from down the street as he jogged to catch up to where Carlos had stopped.

No, no, no. His first official day as a bona fide Californian was turning into a shit show. Amazed at how quickly his anticipation to get to work had soured, all he wanted to do was return to his condo and lose himself inside a painting.

Chapter Three

Well, this wasn't the way Clay had seen his day going, but he'd roll with it. Being tour guide wasn't in his job description or on his friend-favor list, but for the crew at The Gates, he'd make time. They'd welcomed him when he first arrived, inviting him to a barbeque shortly after he'd begun to work out of the DTLA station.

"Wait up, man," he hollered. Carlos wasn't making Clay's attempt at doing a good deed any easier. "What the hell. Do you want a tour guide or not?" he asked the big guy's back as he continued to walk away.

"No, I don't," he replied. "Please go away."

"Your brother wanted me to show you around. What's with the silent treatment? You were plenty talkative at the wedding."

"I was drunk."

No, he wasn't. Clay had noticed Carlos had been drinking bottled water all night.

"You weren't drunk. Nosy, fuck yeah. Drunk, not even close."

Clay had done his best to ignore Carlos when earlier he'd walked through the lounge area at The Gates. No more psychoanalysis from a stranger, fuck you very much. Clay had tagged along with Sam after work and went to The Gates for a late lunch. Then in the damn office, Clay forced himself from turning to face Carlos. This shit had to stop.

As they continued down the sidewalk, getting further away from The Gates with every step, Clay couldn't help but notice a few people openly staring at Carlos. It caught Clay off guard. Some appeared curious, others frightened, but most were sizing him up. Sure, he was a tall man, but the scrutiny wasn't cool.

Even though Carlos was solid and well defined, he wasn't pumped up. Most likely, his scar drew as much attention as his size. That fucker wrapped around his neck and made an already imposing guy look mean and scary.

Clay watched Carlos as he slowly closed in on himself. He lowered his head and raised his collar, then hunched his shoulders to appear smaller. By the time Clay had finally caught up with him and could see his face, he looked a minute away from having a panic attack.

Drawing on his training, Clay came up beside him and took hold of Carlos's arm before leading him off to the side to under a small marquis for an old boarded-up theater.

When Carlos didn't fight him or argue, Clay became more concerned and considered calling Miguel.

"I'm okay. I'm fine," Carlos said repeatedly, and Clay wondered if it was for his benefit the big guy was repeating the mantra.

"Yeah, you are," Clay said, keeping his voice modulated, trying to push calm into his tone and manner. His mother used to call him her tranquilizer because his voice always soothed her when his dad went on one of his benders. "You're safe. No one will get near you with me around. I promise." He had no idea why he said that last bit, but it was true.

"I'm sorry," Carlos muttered between gasps as it seemed he was trying to regulate his breathing. "Thought I was ready."

"You have no reason to be sorry." The guy had no more control over his size than how people reacted. "Is there anything I can do to help?"

Carlos leaned back against the worn stone façade of the old building before finally looking at Clay. "Thanks, man. What you're doing right now has helped."

Carlos's sorrowful blue eyes dealt a sucker punch straight to Clay's chest, causing him to take a step back. He quickly brushed off his reaction by looking around as if that's what he'd intended to do.

"You let me know when you want to try again, and I'll be right beside you," Clay assured as he adjusted his body to block a couple onlookers' view. "Take your time. No one's going to bug you."

"Yeah. Thanks." Carlos lowered his gaze to his camera. "Maybe we should give up for the day."

"If that's what you want to do," Clay shrugged, "sure. But you'll miss out on my world-class tour guide services. With my specially honed skills, I can find the nearest drug den within a mile radius—or a donut shop, whichever you'd prefer." Clay had no idea why he was trying to be funny, but he felt he had to make Carlos smile.

When the big lug did, Clay did as well.

"Officer Everett, I'd advise you not to quit your day job." Carlos gave him a small smile as his body began to uncurl, and his shoulders straightened.

"Pretty bad, huh?"

"Horrible," Carlos huffed before giving a full smile. Everything felt right again. The guy had a great smile.

"So, you wanna take those pictures?" Clay asked, and Carlos looked around as if deciding how much more he could take. "I'll be tagging along if you don't mind."

Clay hated when things were forced on him, and he imagined Carlos felt the same way. Though why he felt invested in this guy's wellbeing beyond usual human kindness was something he'd have to examine later. Or not.

Carlos's eyes squinted, and his eyebrows scrunched tight. "Why are you being nice to me?"

"Because I'm not an asshole," Clay said, though their first meeting and prior behavior might have suggested otherwise. "You need pictures, and I want to help you get them. I'm more familiar with the area than you are, and it's no skin off my back to walk around for a few minutes."

Carlos's expression changed. "Look, I'm sorry for barging into your evening like that at the wedding. I had no right to say what I did."

"I'm sorry for being a shit." Clay figured if the big guy was fessin' up, he would too. "I wasn't at my best."

"Don't like weddings?"

"Something like that," Clay answered. "Tell me what you're looking to take pictures of, and I'll lead the way." Carlos smirked at Clay's quick subject change, and didn't push for why he detested weddings.

After taking a deep breath, Carlos stood straight, or at least as close as possible, while still attempting to appear smaller. The ease at which he did it confirmed it was a conditioned response to people's reaction to him. That had to stop, but not today. Today, they would walk calmly, next time Clay would—wait. What next time? Why was he making plans? He didn't even know the guy.

"Okay."

"Okay?"

"Yeah, you can come along."

"Great." Clay meant it. "Now, where to next? Oh, and there's an extra fee if I have to carry anything."

"Duly noted, officer." Carlos chuckled. "I intended to wander until something caught my eye."

"Your brother said this was for your work. What do you do?" Clay thought he was asking a simple question, but the change in Carlos's expression suggested differently.

"I paint."

"Okay, paint as in walls or art?"

The big guy turned to look at him. "You're one of a small minority that would have even considered the second. I'm an artist."

Carlos stood staring at Clay as if waiting for something. "Are you famous? I'm not trying to be rude, but I don't know squat about the art world." Maybe Clay should know who Carlos was. Thankfully they began walking again.

"It's not that," Carlos said. "You didn't question how someone like me could be an artist."

"Someone like you?" There was more to that statement than whatever answer he was going to get.

"The big, bad wrestler, or bodyguard, whichever way you see me. 'Delicate' isn't a word used to describe me." Carlos held out his large hand. "This couldn't possibly create works that hang in galleries and private collections."

Clay rightly felt guilty that that had been his assumption when they'd first met at the wedding. Imagine being misjudged your entire life. Yep, he was an asshole.

"What do you paint?" Clay wanted to steer the conversation to happier thoughts to keep Carlos calm through the crowds on the street corner.

"Anything that interests me," Carlos replied as he brought his camera up to his eye and took a picture of the packed street.

"What interests you about that scene?" Clay asked, genuinely curious how a street covered in bumper-to-bumper traffic complete with honking horns and teeming with people trying to talk over each other was something beautiful to paint. All he saw was concrete and filth. No doubt he was jaded.

"The flow of all the different people, shapes, and colors that are being lorded over by stone and metal leviathans is intriguing to me.

I'm considering starting a new series of paintings set in urban environments as I've already explained to Max, who asked the same question."

"So flowers and gardens are out," Clay asked as he thought of more areas that might interest Carlos in the city.

"For what I wish to accomplish, yeah," Carlos said. "What about you? Did you always want to be a police officer?"

"No, not from the beginning, but life has a way of showing you the way." Or, in his case, the need for people like him in law enforcement.

"What did you want to be when you were a kid?" Carlos asked.

"A race car driver." Clay couldn't help but smirk at his memories of building cars out of boxes his mom used to bring home from her grocery store job and pretend he was racing, at least until his dad burned them in the pit. "Did you always want to paint?"

Carlos stopped again and took several pictures of a traffic-light pole covered in layers of posters, paper, tape, and staples. Everything from jazz night over at the Rhythm Room on Sixth Street, to some shmucks who lost a boa constrictor and were stupid enough to post signs with a picture of the snake.

"I always dreamed of working with horses, but as I continued to grow, I realized a career involving horseback riding wasn't suited for me or the poor horse. I went with my second choice, painting."

Clay had to agree that Carlos's height and weight, which he guessed was two-hundred and eighty pounds, probably more, wouldn't be comfortable for an average quarter horse.

"Were you always a good artist? Did it come naturally for you, or did you have to work at it?" Clay couldn't stop with the questions. For some reason, he wanted to know more about the man.

"Actually, a bit too naturally," Carlos said, and his voice lowered a couple of octaves.

When Clay turned to look at him to clarify the comment, Carlos had his camera stuck to his face again, taking a picture of a flowering weed sticking out of a crack in the sidewalk. Seriously?

"You have got to show me these paintings when they're done," Clay said. He had to see where Carlos's vision took him. As he was mulling the possibilities over, their conversation was interrupted by an angry voice.

"Get outta the way, asshole," the voice growled. "Fucking taking pictures of a weed. Freak."

On the other side of Carlos stood two teenage boys out to make a name for themselves. There was plenty of room to go around, but these two wanted attention, and they were going to get it.

Clay came to stand beside Carlos, who was already backing away. "You gotta problem?"

"Yeah, bigfoot here is in our way," the taller one with the facial tattoo laughed.

"Go around," Clay said as he motioned to the open sidewalk on either side of them.

Carlos reached for Clay's arm. "It's okay. We can move."

"Are you done taking your pictures?" At Carlos's uncertain look, Clay had his answer. "You go ahead and finish up what you need to get done. Then we'll move."

"You'll move now," the shorter one with the black leather band around his neck said while cocking his arm back and letting his fist fly.

Clay moved to protect Carlos when the big guy's hand shot out in front of them both, catching the fist in the palm of his hand. The shock on both teenagers' faces had to mirror his own.

"I don't want to fight," Carlos growled as he held the fist in place.

Before the two got any more ideas, Clay pulled out his badge. "Leave now."

Carlos released the guy's hand, and both teens took off running in the opposite direction without looking back. Before Clay could say a word, Carlos was already on the move.

He quickly caught up. "Hey, man. You okay?" Maybe Clay should've moved out of the way.

***

Carlos continued walking. Emotions banged against the inside of his chest. Of course he was angry those guys decided to target him, but more than anything, he was shocked Clay had stood up for him. Other than his brother, no one had done that before, not even his foster parents.

"I'm fine. Really. I think I've got enough pictures to get me started on a few ideas." It was time to go home.

Clay took hold of Carlos's arm, making him stop and look at Clay. "Are you sure you're okay? Should I have handled that differently?"

Of course, he should've handled it differently, dammit., but the last thing Carlos wanted to do was make Clay feel guilty for trying to help. This kind of shit seemed to follow Carlos unbidden.

"I'm sure. You didn't do anything wrong. Thanks for defending me."

"By the looks of things, you can defend yourself."

"I don't like violence."

"Yeah, okay, I understand that."

They walked in silence for two more blocks before The Gates came into view, and for some unknown reason, Carlos hadn't noticed a single person staring at him. When they arrived outside the building, Carlos was wracking his brain to find a plausible reason for them to see each other again.

"How about next time I take you to Little Tokyo, and we can take a walk over there while you take pictures?" Clay asked. "If you want to get a sense for DTLA, you need to visit the areas that make it unique."

Carlos was stunned but managed to say, "You're right. I need to see the neighborhoods." Thankfully, Clay had come up with a reason to meet again because Carlos had been drawing a blank.

"It's a date. How's Sunday?" Clay asked.

"Um…good," Carlos stuttered. Clay made decisions fast. Carlos guessed it came with his job. What did Clay mean by "date?"

"I'll pick you up here at nine in the morning," Clay said before turning and crossing the street, heading to the parking garage.

Carlos wasn't sure how long he stood there, but eventually, he managed to make his way back up to his condo. When he found himself standing in the center of his studio buzzing with energy and a need to create, he pulled out his new sketchbook and was ready to make that first mark to the pristine paper and begin anew.

Chapter Four

He'd lost his damn mind. There was no other logical explanation. Clay slammed the refrigerator door with a bit more force than necessary. *It's a date.* Of all the words he could have used, he'd chosen that one. What had he been thinking? He *wasn't* thinking, that was the problem. Whenever he was around Carlos, Clay couldn't think straight.

Little Tokyo. The offer was out of his mouth before he even had a chance to consider it, and now he was saddled with playing tour guide for the day. Clay tried to be angry about that but couldn't. He was looking forward to it.

This whole getting to know someone was doomed to fail. He of all people should remember even something as innocuous as making a new friend was another emotional trap, set to snare him if he got to close. In the end, as it always did, he'd be left feeling humiliated. That shit wasn't going to happen this time around. The old memories tried to rush in, but Clay slammed that door shut.

He walked out of the 1970s-style breakroom complete with a two-pot coffee maker so thoroughly stained you couldn't be sure how much coffee was in the pots unless you shook them, and a microwave that cooked like one of those ovens little girls played with. A mug of rot-gut coffee in hand, he returned to his wood laminate desk to deal with the unfinished reports that'd been gunny-sacked. It'd gotten so bad, Captain Myers placed him and Sam on desk duty until they got caught up. Clay shouldn't complain considering the captain had given them two prior warnings.

Clay set his coffee on his desk, looked at his computer screen, and rubbed his temples with his fingers. Six straight hours of paperwork so far and his eyes were about to cross. He couldn't imagine having a job that required him to be in an office all day, every day. He'd go insane.

With a quick look around to make sure no one was paying any attention, Clay opened his browser and typed in "Carlos Fernandez art." He hadn't had the opportunity to satisfy his curiosity and was eager to check out Carlos's work for himself.

Clay was more than a little shocked when his browser was filled with results. Headlines like, "The Rising Star in Modern Impressionism," "Impressionism for the Twenty-first Century," "Reclusive Artist Taking the Art World by Storm." He went ahead and clicked on a photo of one of Carlos's paintings. His screen filled with light and bright colors.

When he'd imagined painting and artwork, Clay had a preconceived style in mind, something along the line of portraits, or mountains and scenery he'd seen in homes and on television. What did he know? He was a cop, not an art critic. But these—whoa. These were something else. These paintings jumped off the screen and grabbed him.

The brushstrokes were varied: odd and choppy in some places, or short and thin in others. The scenes weren't quite finished in the way he expected, all polished and perfect like he'd seen on walls in homes that were crime scenes No, these were rough, without defining the facial features of the woman in the garden with her child running in the sunlight. But as course as the details were, the setting was captured perfectly. Clay could feel the warmth of the day on the little boy's face.

The next work showed an empty lane overgrown with vegetation reclaiming what once was a paved road. The flowers seemed to rise to touch the sunlight as they swayed in the breeze.

These weren't the calming and gentle scenes he'd imagined. They were raw and real and were stunning and unapologetic in their honesty.

"You suddenly into art?" Sam asked from behind his left shoulder. Clay had been so absorbed in the paintings he hadn't heard his partner come up behind him.

"Maybe," Clay replied.

Sam leaned in closer. "Carlos Fernandez. I see you're looking into The Gates's most recent resident."

"I'm not looking into the guy," Clay said while closing the browser and returning to the LAPD report screen. "He's a painter, and I wanted to see his work. Curiosity, nothing more."

"Looks impressive to me," Sam said. "I still find it hard to believe those sausage fingers can create such intricate pieces."

"Why, because he doesn't fit the mold of an artist? Just because he's bigger than the average person doesn't mean he can't create masterpieces. You of all people know it's important to look under the surface, or you would've stayed away from your boyfriend, Joey." Clay was pissed, the same as he'd been when the people on the street began staring at Carlos. No one had the right to judge him.

"Easy, buddy," Sam said as he raised his hands and took a step back. "Glad to see you have the big guy's back."

"What?"

"I had to check, man." Sam chuckled. "Joey and Carlos have become friends, and we look out for him."

"You were testing me?" Clay asked, pissed off as all hell. "Asshole."

"You're not exactly known for your friendliness," Sam huffed. "Don't get me wrong, you're a great guy, stand-up officer and friend, but when it comes to dating, you're more of a love 'em and leave 'em type."

"What the actual fuck you talking about, man? I don't do that shit."

"That, right there. That attitude. Not cool, man. Carlos is different." Sam pointed at Clay using the file in his hand. "You can't fuck with him like the others. He doesn't do Grindr."

"You're giving me the talk?" Clay almost choked on his tongue. "We're adults."

"If I have to," Sam stated. "Being adults is not an endorsement for good behavior,"

"I'm his tour guide, that's all. You can drop the big brother routine."

"Be thankful I'm not Miguel."

"What's the big deal? He's an adult, and so am I, unless Carlos has a mental impairment I'm not aware of, we're fine." Clay hadn't recognized him as having any, but you can never discount the possibility. He'd never take advantage of anyone. He knew how that felt.

"No, it's more of social impairment. Carlos hasn't been around the block. Hell, he hasn't even turned the first corner."

Clay was beginning to understand what Sam was trying to say. Don't mess with the man's emotions, which was easy since Clay didn't do feelings.

"Look, I'm not trying to take the guy to bed," Clay said a bit loudly, causing a few of their fellow officers to turn and look at them. "Fuck. I'm taking him around the city to take pictures."

"Okay, okay, if that's what you say, man, I believe you." Sam leaned against Clay's desk.

"Done all the reports already?" The captain said from behind both of them. "I'm sure if I look hard enough, I can find a few more the two of you have missed."

Sam hung his head. "Do you have eyes everywhere?" Sam and the captain had been friends for a long time. "Or is it witchcraft? You can tell me, boss."

"More like a quarterly review hanging over my head," the captain said with a grumble. "When they get off my back, I'll get off yours."

"Fine," Sam groaned before rounding Clay's desk and sitting down at his own. "If I get carpal tunnel and can't move my hand it's on you."

"Wouldn't you need to start typing for that to happen?" Clay jabbed.

"Don't think you're off the hook, Everett," Captain Meyers stated. "You're only a quarter of the way through your half. There's no time to use the PD's computer to troll your favorite websites."

"Yes, sir," Clay agreed as Sam shot him an evil grin, the bastard. He liked his work colleagues and considered them friends. This back and forth banter was part of their communication. Cops. Not a touchy-feely group.

Clay pulled up the next report and began reviewing the information and comparing it to his notes. He'd ensure every "i" was dotted, and every "t" was crossed, but in the back of his mind, the few paintings of Carlos's Clay had managed to see took up residence in his mind, and he couldn't find the will to stop thinking about them and the man who created them.

***

With each brushstroke, Carlos's newest painting had come to life. He'd spent days drawing the composition until his vision was clear in his mind, and then confidently, he picked up a paintbrush.

The buildings soared into the sky on either side of the pavement while people and vehicles jockeyed for position. Some features were more apparent than others as their motion dictated, and the bright, thin Los Angeles sunlight flowed over them. The feeling of abundance and happiness in the places where the Californian sunshine touched stood in stark contrast to the darker, more dramatically painted areas where the underbelly of the city lurked. All of it his impression of this single moment on a DTLA street. The feelings of wonder and fear occupied the same space on the canvas as in Carlos's mind.

He'd move on to his second piece tomorrow, but for now he sat back staring at this first painting in a series with a critical eye. The brushes had been cleaned and carefully put away, in an attempt to discourage himself from attempting to "tweak" his work. It was an old habit, much like the others he was trying to program out of himself.

The same two voices echoed through his head on repeat and Carlos was having a hard time shutting them out. *That's not good enough. Work harder. You're not finished until it's perfect. If it weren't for us, you'd have died in the gutter where we found you. Show some respect. We need more money. Work faster, you ingrate.*

Carlos had tried to silence them, but with the move to a new city and a new condo, and meeting so many people, his nerves were on edge. He'd been unsuccessful in putting his mental demons back in a box. They were berating him, demanding more from him than any one person could do. His muscles tensed as the voices blended into a crushing crescendo dangling above him.

"Carlos?"

Even though the voice was familiar, it didn't temper his response. He jumped from his chair, sending it flying out behind him and turned, arms up, fists raised. He'd die before going back.

"Easy, brother," Miguel hollered as he quickly dodged the chair. "It's only me."

"Miguel?"

"Yeah, man."

Carlos could feel the adrenaline still racing through his body as he lowered his arms. "You scared the shit out of me. What're you doing in my apartment?"

"You left the door unlocked. Again. I called your name a couple of times from the doorway and you didn't answer," Miguel grumbled.

"Oh."

"Yeah, oh," Miguel said as he lifted the folding chair from the floor. "You trying to kill me with this?"

Carlos shook out his tense arms and said, "No. I was trying to slow down whoever was coming at me so I could defend myself."

Miguel's expression changed from anger to concern. "They can't ever get near you again."

"We hope." There was always a chance.

"Thick metal bars assure that they won't."

"Not forever." Unfortunately, there was a thing called parole.

"No, not forever, but you're not the same person you were then."

"Weak."

"You were never weak," Miguel growled. "They took advantage of you because you had no other choice. You were a child."

Often Carlos felt more like that child than the man he'd become. Desperate for acceptance and love, but knowing he'd never receive it. True, it had been years since he'd seen his foster parents, but their memory lived on in his nightmares.

It was time for a different subject. Carlos had spent enough time dealing with the damage they'd done for today. "What's up? Visiting?"

"I've been busy the last four days with the third floor, and I wanted to check in with you. Did you just finish this?" Miguel asked as he stepped closer to Carlos's painting. "It's powerful, brother."

"What do you see when you look at it?" Carlos asked. He'd always been curious about what others saw in his paintings, why they'd want to buy them and put them up in their houses or in their collections.

Miguel took a few steps closer, and Carlos joined his brother to look at his painting. Miguel didn't answer right away. He took his time, his head tilting in consideration of what he was seeing. Miguel had always taken Carlos's work seriously, which made him more likely to ask his brother's opinion. He'd be lying if he said he wasn't nervous to hear what Miguel had to say. Carlos's art was a part of him, like his hand or leg, physically connected in all the ways that mattered.

"I see the dichotomy between hope and the backdrop of the city's reality all under the watchful eye of those in power." As he spoke, Miguel gestured to the lighter areas first, then the darker ones and the tall buildings set as bookends to the subjects below. "The essence of Los Angeles, I'd say."

Carlos couldn't help his smile. He loved that his brother got him. Of course, he understood each person who saw the painting would come away with a different opinion and impression, but his brother understood what he saw.

"By your smile, I take it you're happy with this one," Miguel said while motioning between the completed work and the rough sketches strewn across the bench.

"I am," Carlos said. The voices had gone silent, and his head felt lighter.

"If this is any indication, I'm going to like your new urban series. It's grittier," Miguel said. "Right up my alley."

"Thanks, man." His brother's approval meant more to him than anything. "Want something to drink?"

"You got beer?" Miguel's eyebrows shot up.

"What do you think?" Carlos laughed as he headed down the hall to his still unpacked kitchen.

"So when are you getting around to unboxing the rest of your stuff?" Miguel asked as he weaved his way through the piles.

"I'll get to it eventually. As long as I can work, I'm happy," Carlos answered. "I have this IPA from Firestone called Flyjack. I like it. Wanna try one?" He liked the crisp taste and how light it was, along with the hint of citrus.

"Serve 'em up, brother." Miguel removed boxes from the couch and chairs while Carlos grabbed two beers from his fully stocked fridge. He'd had his groceries delivered so he didn't have to go out. Between Grubhub, Instacart, and Uber Eats, ordering groceries, cleaning supplies, and household stuff had made it possible for Carlos to avoid going out.

He knew it was cheating, considering how he'd said he wanted to step back into the world, but he had been painting and couldn't take the time away from his work to shop for himself. *Keep telling yourself that.*

By the time Carlos reached the living room, Miguel had already set up the area rug, couch, and two chairs, along with the coffee table and floor lamps. The Marine couldn't abide disorder.

"Here," Carlos said as he held out a can of beer to his brother. "Thanks for setting this up."

"No problem, that's what family's for," Miguel said before taking a deep swig and sitting down on the couch. "Where's your TV?"

"I don't have one."

"What? Why?" Miguel stuttered.

"Never had one. Don't see the purpose. I have a laptop." Carlos's foster parents had a TV, but he wasn't allowed to watch it.

He sat in one of the chairs and set his beer down on the coffee table. That he was sitting in his living room drinking a beer with his brother was a moment not lost on him.

"This is nice," Miguel said, obviously thinking on the same wavelength.

"Something we need to do often," Carlos agreed.

"I hear Clay's help earlier this week went so well that the two of you are doing it again on Sunday."

"Yeah. He's taking me to Little Tokyo." Carlos was looking forward to wandering through the neighborhood and had begun researching online. He wanted to dig into the culture and was surprised to learn the history of the area dated back to the late 1800s.

"Okay, but if you need me for any reason, I'm only a call away," Miguel told him.

Carlos shook his head. "I'm a grown man, bro. Though I appreciate the offer, I'll be fine with Clay."

"I know you are. But you gotta admit some social situations are still difficult for you. If Clay pressures you—"

"Oh my god, if you're about to start in with an 'It's okay to say no' speech, I'm going to chuck this can at your head," Carlos threatened.

"But—"

Carlos lifted his can.

"Okay, okay. Got it. Stay out of your personal life."

"No. I want you in my personal life. You're my brother, and I love you. But even though I've spent most of my life in solitude, that doesn't mean I'm naïve. If I don't want something to happen, it won't." He smirked. "If I do, that's my business."

"Understood," Miguel said as he lifted his can. "I'd like to propose a toast. May the brothers Fernandez always stick their noses into each other's lives even if it doesn't belong."

"Here, here," Carlos raised his can in salute and took a long pull on his beer.

Chapter Five

Little Tokyo was roughly five city blocks bracketed by four streets: Los Angeles, Alameda, Third, and First. The area had been made into a National Historic Landmark District sometime back in the nineties.

They'd left Clay's car in a parking garage across from The Gates. Little Tokyo wasn't far and they'd be walking. Carlos had packed his messenger bag with his camera, memory card, pencils, and his sketchbook for the day's adventure. He'd hoped to find the subject of at least one more painting in his new series, but it was never a guarantee. For him to choose an image, it had to cause a physical and emotional response.

He was nervous, He didn't want a repeat performance of his last outing, and he'd battled through a rough night with little sleep. But when he'd rushed out of the front doors of The Gates this morning and saw Clay waiting for him, an odd tingle raced through his body at the sight of the handsome man leaning against the light pole with his legs crossed at the ankle. Those mesmerizing eyes locked on his every move. Carlos knew there wasn't a chance for anything romantic to happen between them, but a guy could fantasize. Clay had already taken the starring role in Carlos's daydreams. He wouldn't be surprised if Clay showed up in nighttime dreams as well.

Without saying a word, Carlos joined him, and Clay held out one of two to-go coffee containers filling the air with the heavenly aroma of roasted Arabica beans. After a morning that found him racing for the front door after spending at least thirty minutes looking for his spare memory card, Carlos felt a calm settle over him. That was twice now that that had happened in Clay's presence. The man was a giant Prozac. Though Carlos doubted Clay would appreciate the comparison, the peace meant more than he could say.

When they hit the streets, there weren't many people walking around, and Carlos began to relax a bit more as they made their way to Little Tokyo and began their tour.

"How are you feeling so far?" Clay asked, making Carlos smile. "Anxiety level okay?"

"Yeah," Carlos replied. "The day began better than I'd expected."

"With me as your tour guide, how could you have ever had a doubt?" Clay joked. "And wait, there's more."

"The anticipation is killing me," Carlos shot back with a laugh.

"Then follow me," Clay said with his left eyebrow raised.

Small shops lined the walkways while red and white paper lanterns rocked back and forth above them from the slight breeze in the open shopping area. A wooden arch, or torii, as he'd learned, declared that they were indeed in Little Tokyo.

An impressive and solid-looking wood beam watchtower stood tall outside the Japanese Village Plaza, and a brick walkway with stone benches, potted bushes, and small trees dotted their path. There were sidewalk cafés, sushi joints, ramen bars, traditional and modern clothing stores, makeup and anime shops, and vending machines stuffed full of prizes featuring games like the Claw.

His gaze roamed in all directions trying to take in the rich colors, Japanese writing and art, the scents and aromas, and the feeling that in this little place, he was somewhat transported to another country. Carlos hadn't explored much. He'd take his pictures and get out of wherever he was without causing an incident. His actions mimicked the internal mantra—get in, get out, get home. Now, though, he found himself wanting to wander into those shops and sit in a café drinking coffee and watching people walk by.

Across the street, there was a vintage clothing store, and another shop displaying rows of lucky waving cats in different colors. There were a couple of sweets shops that'd been there for over a hundred years, and Carlos wouldn't mind visiting them.

The delicious aromas wafting out from the nearby restaurants were tempting him to come in for a bite, but they were heading to the Japanese American Cultural and Community Center first. Indulging would have to wait.

Carlos hadn't had enough time to research a lot about the Center as his concentration had been mainly on the shops and streets, but he was eager to have a look inside. There was also a place in Weller Court, a three-story open-air shopping plaza nearby, that Carlos wanted to visit. According to his internet searches, Books Kinokuniya had an array of books from text to art, magazines, stationery, manga, you name it, and Carlos wanted to wander its aisles and get lost among the colorful pages.

He wasn't sure if that was on the day's schedule, but Clay had asked Carlos if there was anywhere specific he wanted to go, so there was always a chance he'd get to indulge his senses.

When they entered the community center, Clay went to the left and signed them in before leading Carlos to the elevators.

"We aren't going to check out the workshops or displays?" Carlos asked, disappointed that he couldn't have a closer look at these first rooms.

"There's something I'd like to show you first," Clay answered before stepping into the elevator and pushing the button with a "B" on it. They went down a level, and followed a hallway until they reached an oasis that stood amidst the stone and metal of the city.

"This is the James Irvine Japanese Garden," Clay announced as he opened his arms wide to encompass the scene in front of them. "I thought this might be the best way to kick off our day of sightseeing."

Carlos took a long look around before saying, "You're right."

Trees in bloom were surrounded by bushes and plants of alternating sizes filling the garden with texture and beauty. There was a footpath lined with stones, and two bridges traversed a stream that ended in a pond. The setting was calm and quiet. Only the sound of rushing water from the waterfall echoed through the space. Stone pagodas, and metal and paper lanterns adorned the multi-level garden.

Multiple shades of green sprinkled with brightly-colored blooms teased the eye as the rocks and water grounded the entire scene. A truly gorgeous and unexpected treat. What caught Carlos's interest the most was the slow shift in the view as his sightline travelled higher, and slim snippets of reality came into focus in the form of various buildings looming in the background of this hidden treasure.

If he kept his gaze cast downward, he imagined he was someplace else far from DTLA. This garden was the heart of this area, buried deep beneath the landscape. Protected. Loved.

"This place is surreal. I have no words."

The flowing water drew him closer and his fingers itched to take photos. Then it hit him that this would be the ideal place to try *plein air* painting again. He'd have to think about the mechanics of doing it before attempting it again. Last time had been a complete failure, but he was focused on the future, which was beginning to look brighter by the hour.

***

Clay sat back and watched as Carlos moved fluidly through the space, the camera his artist's eye, same as the first time Clay watched him work. Carlos had straightened to his full height, forgetting about the people around him. He allowed himself to explore and opened up to the visual wealth around him. His art was his portal to society while he remained a safe distance away, working alone, withdrawn from the world he captured so well.

Clay wondered what'd happened to cause Carlos's extreme reaction to and fear of people. The big guy was as gentle as they came, even if the scar circling his throat told a different story. The thought of anyone hurting him ignited the bubbling anger and ever-present protectiveness that lay beneath Clay's surface, as nothing else had in years. The last time was the day they took his old man away for his third stint behind bars.

Carlos was a puzzle, and the more Clay knew, the more he wanted to know. Clay had spent the entire week trying to dull his heart's reaction to Carlos only to have his efforts fly out the damn window the moment he laid eyes on him this morning. Even now, as he sat on one of the stone benches staring at the concrete lantern in the stream in front of him, Clay couldn't get his heart to beat regularly, and the fizzing in his stomach was nowhere near under control.

The happiness he'd seen on Carlos's face was a drug to which Clay was quickly becoming addicted.

So deep in his head, Clay hadn't noticed Carlos had moved closer until the scrape of shoes against dirt caused Clay to look up to find Carlos taking pictures of him. "Hey, we're here for the flowers and trees, not the weeds."

"You're no weed," Carlos said before snapping one last picture.

"I wouldn't be so sure of that," Clay grumbled. "You don't know me well enough."

"I want to," Carlos mumbled, then looked abashed for having said it.

Clay couldn't stop the smile that broke over his face. "So would I." The words came out of his mouth unbidden. It would seem he and Carlos were suffering from the same condition, and Clay would be damned if his cheeks weren't warming. The happiness that transformed Carlos's expression was worth Clay's embarrassment. "You get all the pictures you want?"

"Yeah." Carlos's answer came out gravelly, and he cleared his throat before he continued. "Thanks for bringing me here. An unexpected treasure."

"I'm glad you liked it," Clay said. "You getting hungry? We can stop for something to eat. Café Dulce serves a delicious vegetarian breakfast burrito."

"I'd like that." Carlos nodded. "I could use a bit more coffee."

Clay smiled. "Come on. This way to sustenance."

It took only a few minutes to walk over to the café. Little Tokyo was only a few square blocks. They took a seat outside in the warming sun as Carlos continued to snap pictures of their surroundings. So far, only a couple of people gave him a second look. Other than that, things were going a whole lot smoother than Clay imagined they would. Then again, things had run pretty well the last time once the big guy calmed down.

Without the whole awkward phase of their first initial outing, everything seemed to come naturally, and Clay relaxed into it.

After they'd ordered their burritos and coffee Clay decided to get nosy. "So you and Miguel are brothers?"

"Half-brothers. We have the same mom," Carlos answered as he snapped a picture of the small vase on the table containing a single purple orchid.

"I'm sorry to hear about your mother's death." Clay remembered Miguel's parents had died in a car accident. Carlos nodded. "From what I hear, you were kind of a surprise to the Gates crew since Miguel hadn't mentioned he had a brother." *Great. A subtle icebreaker.*

Thankfully, Carlos didn't seem bothered by Clay's probing.

"We'd first met in our early twenties at the funeral. Our mom was young when she got pregnant with me and her parents gave me away shortly after I was born. Back then, parents sent their pregnant daughters to other towns because it was an embarrassment to their family."

"That had to be rough on you and your mom." Clay had often wished for new parents as a child, and he thought of how unfair emotional distribution was universally. From Carlos's expression, he would've preferred to have been raised by his mother, and Clay had been stuck with people who had no business being parents.

Carlos nodded and looked to be considering his next words carefully. "I was put into the foster care system and stayed there until I was eighteen."

"How were your foster parents?" Clay asked.

"Not as good as you'd hope," Carlos answered.

"Look, you don't have to tell me a thing if you don't want to. We all have shit buried away for one reason or another." Clay thought about his demons and decided it was time for some quid pro quo. "My family lived in East Hollywood. It was a working-class neighborhood and rough around the edges. Street crimes were daily events, and everyone locked up everything they owned, or it'd be taken soon enough."

"That doesn't sound like a safe place for a kid to grow up," Carlos said, his tone soft.

"I was young. What did I know? I played in the streets and on sidewalks because no one had a yard. The park was where the junkies went to score and shoot up, so it was safer on the streets. Violence was commonplace, and the sounds of sirens barely registered as an event around there." Clay shoved aside the emotions that came along with memories before they had a chance to affect him. Those memories, along with the people, were dead and buried—most of the time.

Carlos grunted. "Once my foster parents discovered my talent, I wasn't allowed out of the house anymore. I was eleven."

"What the hell. Why?"

"They didn't want me to get away," Carlos explained with a curious lack of emotion.

"Get away?" Clay wasn't liking the direction of this conversation. "What talent did you have at eleven years old?"

"Painting."

"Yes, I know you're an artist. I've even looked up your work. I'm going to need a bit more than that to go on."

"You did. Did you like the paintings you saw?"

"Yep. The paintings are great. Back to the subject. What about your painting was important to them?" Maybe they were selling his art as their own and making a hell of a profit.

Carlos took a deep breath, looked around to see if anyone was listening, and said, "I can recreate any painting or picture I see."

"Shit."

"Yeah. I was too young to know any better. My foster parents had me painting forgeries of mainly mid-range artists to make money while keeping a low profile."

"How did you get away?"

"Years later, a new social worker was assigned to my case. The previous one had been getting a percentage of the profits to keep her mouth shut, at least until a car accident forced her off on disability."

"What happened when they found out what your foster parents were forcing you to do?" As far as Clay was concerned, there wasn't be a cell deep enough in the earth for people who took advantage of and hurt children.

Before Carlos could answer, their breakfast was delivered along with fresh coffee. When Carlos dug into his food, Clay knew their conversation was at an end. He wasn't discouraged. They'd have time to get to know each other. Hell, he had the whole of DTLA to show Carlos.

Chapter Six

Carlos replaced the cloth covering one of his paintings. He wasn't ready to share the work with anyone, and, in truth, he may never be. Carlos felt the same about it as his other paintings, but this one was more personal. A part of him was tied to it. With a deep sigh, he put the canvas away and returned to his current work.

His trip to Little Tokyo had provided the subjects for two new paintings. One from inside the hidden garden, another of a merchant selling goods along the sidewalk in front of a small store. The day had turned out far better than he had hoped for, and he and Clay were scheduled to visit the Santa Monica Pier together this Saturday.

Recently, Carlos had taken to making regular appearances downstairs at The Gates. Everything was coming together. He'd made friends, spent more time in public, and he had his own handsome personal tour guide. So why the hell did he feel anxious and stay up pacing half the night? There were no threats, no danger, not even a raised voice or scraped knee. He was angry with himself for creating problems when there were none.

He decided to put it down to the stress of the move, and a new place and people. But that didn't seem right. Something deep inside of him had been on the alert the past couple of days, and he couldn't explain it away.

Frustrated and tired, he headed to the master bedroom that he'd managed to organize enough to sleep in. His California king mattress and box spring were placed over a solid wood bedframe built for his proportions and weight. If he'd bought a standard frame, he would've had to replace it every couple of years.

He used the last of his energy to crawl onto the mattress and collapse, his exhaustion finally taking hold, pulling him under into a restless sleep.

When he opened his eyes, he found himself in the last place he'd ever wanted to be: his former room in his foster parents' house. He spun around, taking it all in, the same as he'd remembered it down to the metal screen bolted to the window and the peeling floral wallpaper. He looked at himself in the mirror, wholly expecting to see his younger self staring back at him, but found the grown man he'd become.

This had to be a dream. More like a nightmare. He couldn't be back in this place. He was free. Footsteps came from down the hallway, and he knew the sound of those shoes. His foster dad, Earl, the man who'd made Carlos's life a living hell. He stood to his full height and straightened his back. If the POS wanted a piece of him, he'd gladly oblige. He wasn't the frightened kid he used to be.

But in so many ways, he was. He'd lived most of his free life hiding away from people and not living in the company of society.

The knob turned, and the door flew open, slamming the handle into the busted drywall behind it. Carlos braced himself for attack, but instead watched as his former foster father dragged a younger version of Carlos into the room.

"If you ever try to get away again, I'll break both of your legs," Earl yelled as spittle flew from his chapped lips. "You don't need them to paint, so don't push me. Now get back to work and make sure it's perfect."

Earl threw the young kid onto his unmade bed before stepping back out and pulling the door shut. The click from the padlock confirmed that they were again locked in. Carlos, the adult, emerged from the shadows, not wanting to scare the kid further. It was beyond strange being in the same room as his younger self, even if it was a dream.

"Are you all right?" he asked in the least threatening voice he could muster. The kid had been through enough.

The boy didn't move. Carlos stepped a bit closer. "Hey, kid, are you hurt?"

Still nothing.

By now, he was close enough to touch the child he used to be and reached out for the kid's foot to give it a light tap. "Hey, can you hear me?" When he lowered his finger to the sole of the shoe, it went straight through the old pair of sneakers he remembered pinched his feet because they were too small. He couldn't remember ever wearing clothing that fit.

Taking a shocked step back, he tried reaching for the bare bulb lamp with the same effect. He had no power or form in this nightmare, yet was forced to watch his younger self cry without being able to comfort him. Much the same as the reality he'd lived through. In his sleep, he chastised himself for going back to events he couldn't change.

Carlos realized he'd never been this lucid in one of his dreams. Usually he woke with flashes of memories and shadows, and nothing more. This time, everything was already far too real.

The kid jumped off the bare bed and stormed straight through Carlos, and over to his easel, picked up a pair of scissors along with his latest canvas.

"Do it," Carlos yelled, remembering the emotions raging through the child he used to be. "Destroy it." Anger coursed through his veins.

The French Renaissance recreation shook in the boy's hand as he held the scissors high, ready to plunge them through the canvas. Even though Carlos already knew the outcome, he wished he had the power to change this memory.

Slowly the scissors lowered and fell to the floor as tears gathered in the boy's eyes. He gently placed the canvas back on the easel before he crumpled to the floor beside the scissors Carlos went to his knees and sobbed at the memory that had played out before him. He wept for the boy he was and all he'd lost.

This moment in time had been the tipping point, the day Carlos had surrendered to his fate and given up on any hope that he would ever get away.

He had been broken that day, and in too many ways, he still was.

***

"How's the new series coming?" Brad asked from behind the bar as Carlos was eating his lunch. He'd come down to the lounge to have a bite and to get out of his head. The grilled chicken cobb salad was delicious, and was his new lunchtime favorite.

"Good. I have three paintings completed so far to choose from." He hadn't lacked for inspiration. This city provided so many different backdrops filled with rich culture, people, and locations. He'd never tire from it.

"Choose from?"

"Yeah. I paint first and then curate the collection afterward. That way, I stay in the moment and don't get too caught up in perfection. I don't want my paintings to be perfect. I want them to spark emotions and thoughts." He never wanted to have to paint perfectly ever again.

"That's a cool way of looking at it," Brad said as he finished pouring a draft for another customer.

Carlos noticed Brad shake out his left arm. "How is it?" Brad had been shot in the arm, protecting two police officers, and now one of those officers was his boyfriend.

"Well, PT is over, so I guess the range of motion I have now is all I'm going to get back. But it's much better than where I began." He handed the beer to one of the waiters and adjusted his tinted glasses. "It's the photophobia that's driving me nuts. Who knew a good knock to the head would make the light my enemy?"

"It's gotta suck being sensitive to light and living in LA," Carlos said. "Do the doctors know how long it's going to last?"

"They'd hoped it would have cleared up by now, yet, here I am, Mr. Sunglasses Indoors. I can't even be mistaken for a celebrity because I'm working behind the bar. On to bigger and better things. I hear you and Clay have another date planned for tomorrow," He wiped down the bar-top beside Carlos even though no one had even sat there since the last time he cleaned it.

"I don't think I'd call it a date," Carlos deflected, not wanting people to come to any sort of conclusion just because he and Clay were spending time together.

"He picks you up, you go out on the town, and at some point, you eat. Sounds like a date to me," Brad said as he raised a finger for each event to make his point.

Well, if you looked at it that way, today would be their second date. However, their "outings" lacked the whole romantic element. Carlos never professed to understand relationships, but he assumed there'd be romance.

He pushed his empty plate forward as he thought about what constituted romance. Sex was easy, but when emotions got involved, things became complicated. "Shouldn't there be romance involved if it were a date?"

"I guess," Brad answered. "But, it could be in the little things."

"Little things?" There was nothing little about him—or Clay, for that matter.

"Yeah, like showing you around and hanging out with you," Brad explained. "It doesn't have to be big gestures."

"I've never really had dates before, but I even know that."

"You haven't?"

Uh oh. "I guess not," he said while trying to figure a way out of this conversation. He'd already given away too much. "I had a friend who I was close to physically, but we never went on dates. We'd hang out at my place."

Brad came closer, leaned in, and lowered his voice. "Is that the only man you've ever slept with?"

Carlos was unsure how to answer that in a way he'd come out looking good. The truth made him look pathetic. He knew that. "That's not important. You're supposed to be helping me figure out romance. What does your man, Meyers, do?"

"What doesn't that man do?" Brad's smile turned wicked. "There was this one time I was naked and—"

"Stop." Carlos laughed while covering his ears. "It might be safer if I asked someone else."

"But flowers, melted chocolate, candles, and a butt plug were involved," Brad said earnestly as if he was calling the scene.

"Nope. Nope. That's good. I'm fine," Carlos stammered. "I'll Google it."

Brad's smile never faded. "Well, if you ever need advice, I'm here for you."

"Thanks. I'll remember that." Carlos would never take him up on it, but he appreciated the offer.

Another customer waved at Brad to get his attention. "Gotta go back to work, we'll talk later."

"Okay," Carlos said as he placed his cash under his empty coffee cup. As Brad turned around, Carlos was moving off his barstool and heading for the third floor. He hadn't seen his brother in a few days and wanted to stop by and check in. The restoration work was advancing through the third floor quickly now that the rooms had been framed. Soon they'd be advertising the third floor units for sale and more people would be living here at The Gates.

The amount of detail and care that went into this restoration was unsurpassed by anything he'd ever seen. Down to the last detail, nothing had been overlooked. He could see and feel the pride that the crew had put into it all, many of them craftsmen in their fields. The large replacement windows paid homage to the era the building was erected, and the stunning gates that hung on the interior past the front doors were part of the original building. He could see how wondrous this place must have been in its heyday, the golden age of Hollywood.

The melody of construction noise met him as he stepped off the elevator. Only the owners of the building and the construction supervisor had keys to this floor. Carlos had one because his brother wanted him to have unfettered access if he needed Miguel for any reason.

Carlos followed the sound of people talking, and walked into a unit where they were wiring through the studs to find Max and Miguel in the middle of a discussion while staring at a would-be wall.

"Hey guys," Carlos said as he got closer. "How's it going?"

Both spun around to face him. "Good. You've come out of your painting cave," Miguel joked.

"Yeah. I needed some fresh air. I was getting high on the paint thinner."

"What's up? You look tired," Miguel said. "Working into the wee hours?"

"Something like that," Carlos replied. "Listen, Max, you remember offering me a reference to the same doctor Saint visits weekly? I want to take you up on that."

"What's wrong?" Miguel asked, his brow furrowed.

"I need to get a handle on my nightmares. I used to have a therapist before I moved. I thought I was far enough along to handle this on my own, but clearly not."

"That's why you look so tired," Miguel stated.

"Yeah. Rough couple of nights." He should've never stopped therapy. It'd saved his life.

"I'll get you the phone number," Max said.

"Thanks. I appreciate you doing that for me."

"Maybe it's the added stress of going out," Miguel said as he crossed his arms. "Perhaps if you slowed your advance into public life again, it might help."

"No. I don't think that's it. I felt calm when we went to Little Tokyo."

"Calm?" Max asked, and Miguel uncrossed his arms.

"Yeah. The first time I went out, I was ready to give up, but Clay calmed me enough to get in the pictures I needed. Then, in Little Tokyo, we were walking and hanging out, and I barely paid attention to whether anyone was staring at me."

"He did?" Miguel seemed surprised. "He doesn't strike me as having a soft, calm side."

"Maybe he shows it only to certain people." The thought that perhaps Clay treated him differently made Carlos's chest swell. "I must be one of the lucky ones."

Miguel recrossed his arms. Never a good sign. "I don't want him to take advantage of the situation."

"I do," Carlos huffed, making Max laugh loudly. "I know this is hard for you to believe, but my lack of social skills doesn't mean I'm naïve."

Miguel ran the palm of his hand down his face. "You know, I recently got you back, and it would gut me if something happened to you. Then I'd have to gut the asshole who hurt you. It's a vicious cycle. Do you want me to go to prison?" Miguel's grin assured Carlo his brother was joking.

"It'd give you time to think about all your shortcomings."

"Shit, shortcomings. What shortcomings? I'm perfect," Miguel said as he opened his arms wide and pointed at himself.

"Keep telling yourself that," Carlos shot back.

"You guys kill me," Max laughed again. "Makes me miss not having a sibling."

"You've had to deal with Miguel for years," Carlos said. "You're family."

Max's expression turned serious. "Thanks, man. Means a lot."

"I'll leave you two to your work," Carlos said, turning to head toward the elevator. "The place is looking great, by the way."

"Thanks, bro. Be patient while I try to get this big brother thing under control. Think of it as cramming eighteen years of lording over you into a few months."

"Considering I'm older and the big brother, I'd appreciate that."

"Deal."

With a hearty slap to his shoulder, it seemed that he and Miguel had reached an agreement of sorts. At least for now.

Chapter Seven

Clay couldn't believe what he was reading. He'd been driven by his need to know everything about Carlos, so he began searching for answers. The cop in him was never satisfied until he had the full story. Often he'd wondered if he should plot a course to becoming a detective instead of remaining a patrol cop.

Through an off-the-cuff Q&A with Finn, Clay had learned where Carlos grew up. Everything the big guy had told him about his foster home experience played out in the headlines all those years ago. He'd been sixteen when the new social worker raised the alarm, and the home was raided. Initially, they'd arrested Carlos along with his foster parents for creating the forgeries. He'd spent time in jail until the prosecutor's office finally realized that Carlos was a victim as much as the people who bought the forgeries.

Even though the events had occurred nearly two decades ago, it still read like a good crime novel written today: evil foster parents enslaving a little boy with incredible talent, art forgery, international fraud, the victim sent to jail only to be rescued by a diligent prosecutor, all of which resulted in the boy seeking a life away from the public eye, and the perpetrators going to prison.

Carlos had made a reappearance in his mid-twenties when a gallery held a showing of his works. Along with the adulation came questions about his past and the authenticity of these paintings. To prove that it was indeed his original work, his manager had set up a demonstration for the critics.

They met at a location of the detractors' choosing, and Carlos would then paint *en plein air*, create a painting out in the open air of the area before him. Clay couldn't imagine the position Carlos had been put in, having to prove himself innocent of wrongdoing repeatedly.

Of course, Carlos stood firm and was wholly vindicated when he created a painting called "Lost Innocence." They'd taken him to a rusted and forgotten school playground instead of a more pleasing landscape. Clay couldn't imagine them doing anything to make it a more difficult setting for Carlos, but he rose to the occasion and created something spectacular.

Clay stared at the painting Carlos had created over two days and felt his heart breaking. He imagined the boy inside of Carlos looking longingly at the rusted monkey bars and empty swings. Seeing the simple pleasures denied to him, all while he was painting like a trained seal for the onlookers. Clay was furious even though it happed over a decade ago.

After that, Carlos disappeared back into his self-imposed exile, choosing to communicate through his manager. His paintings found a large following as his reclusive artist reputation grew along with his paintings' worth. Depending on its size, a painting could range anywhere from fifty thousand dollars to three quarters of a million dollars at an art auction or from gallery sales.

Clay was incredibly proud of how far Carlos had come after such horrible beginnings. Still, one question remained: Why had he asked Miguel to keep their familial relationship a secret? Clay had plenty of possible reasons floating around in his mind, but until Carlos told him, he wouldn't know for sure.

He could wait, and would. From what Clay had learned, everything Carlos had done was done with a helluva good reason.

***

The squawk of seagulls, along with the sound of crashing waves soothed Carlos as he dug his toes into the sand and waited for the next cold wash from the Pacific to rush over his feet. The Santa Monica Pier area was touristy but fun. Street performers stood in specifically assigned areas performing magic tricks, creating art, or playing an instrument, among other things. They were spread out enough so people could enjoy one without being interrupted by another. He made sure to leave a tip for each. On either side of the pier were wide beaches with loads of sand, and a coastline that wended its way up through Malibu, enticing surfers, wind-sailers, and volleyball players.

Santa Monica had more restaurants than Carlos had ever seen in one place anywhere, and the variety was astounding. Hungry for

Asian food—what's your pleasure? Vietnamese, Thai, Chinese, Japanese, Korean... Carlos couldn't believe what he was seeing. A few restaurants hung over or lined the ocean, but most were in town, many bracketing the Third Street Promenade.

They'd been in Santa Monica since early afternoon, and it was now approaching seven in the evening. It had been a great day of adventure and photo-taking, leaving him with lots of inspiration for more paintings in his new series. He'd sent a few snaps off to his manager for his opinion about this new direction Carlos was taking and received encouragement, which solidified the feeling he'd had that this was a good place for him to live artistically. The constant concern over who was watching him was no longer a part of his life and was a welcomed relief.

"You getting hungry?" Clay asked from his spot on the sand a few feet away. Carlos had convinced him, after much cajoling, to take off his shoes and sink his feet into the sand at the waterline.

"Sure. I could eat."

"There's a restaurant up on the corner called Del Frisco's Grille. I hear it has great baby-back ribs."

Simply the thought made Carlos's stomach growl in agreement. "That sounds amazing. Lead on, oh fearless um... leader, commander, hmm. That didn't come out right."

"As long as we both know who's leading." Clay laughed, and took hold of Carlos's hand.

The move shocked him, but there was no way Carlos was letting go. *This* was romance. Clay's friendly but stoic outer shell was finally chipping away and Carlos was getting a peek inside at the real man, and he liked what he found. Sure, Clay was a bit gruff, but he was always friendly and helpful while keeping himself at a distance.

They both stood staring off at the horizon with their toes buried in the sand for another couple of minutes before deciding to put their shoes back on and head across the street for dinner.

The arch over the street leading to the Pier was blue and white with yellow accents on either side and read, *Santa Monica Yacht Harbor, Sport Fishing, Boating, Cafes.* He thought it would read Santa Monica Pier. What did he know? The End of the Trail Route 66 sign brought out a bit of nostalgia in him. He'd read about the iconic stretch of highway and the migration out west, particularly after the Dust Bowl, that ran from Chicago across several states and ended in Santa Monica at the Pacific Ocean.

His foster parents had stacks of old magazines from the forties, fifties, and sixties stored in his bedroom. Carlos would dream of the chance to take to the open road, visit small-town America and the Grand Canyon. He'd imagine all the adventures he could take. It'd been the only means of escape left to him.

He and Clay sat at a table out front on the patio so that they could watch the sunset and ordered a couple of drafts before looking over the menu.

"Did you enjoy yourself today?" Clay asked.

"Yeah," Carlos answered. He couldn't wipe the smile from his face if he tried.

A warm breeze came up and ruffled their napkins, but neither he nor Clay had stopped staring at each other. Carlos was drowning in those azure blue depths, and he wasn't fighting it. The waiter returned with their beers, finally breaking their locked gaze.

Carlos took a big gulp of his beer before opening the menu in front of him. "So, you said something about ribs."

Clay chuckled and opened his menu. "I've heard good things."

"Well then, I think we need to try them to confirm what you've heard."

"An investigation of sorts?" Clay played along, and Carlos had to wonder how long it had been since either of them joked around.

"Yes, a ribbing of the ribs you could say."

Clay laughed. It was a deep vibrating sound, and Carlos loved hearing it. "A frisking of the fricassee?"

"Doesn't that have white sauce?" Carlos asked.

"I don't know. It's the best I could come up with on a moment's notice."

"Maybe we could get a lead on the lettuce."

"A snare on the snail."

"Get the goods on the gorgonzola."

The two burst out laughing as the waiter returned for their order. The young man smiled along with them, probably having overheard part of their conversation. "What can I get you tonight, gentlemen? Ribs, chicken fricassee, garden salad, escargot, or a charcuterie board with gorgonzola cheese?"

He'd heard it all. "You're working for that tip tonight, aren't you?" Carlos asked.

Richard—he wore a nametag—grinned.

Clay answered, "All tasty offers, but we're going with the ribs."

"Good choice," he replied.

Carlos was having the best time and didn't want it to end after dinner. "Maybe we could go over to the amusement park before we leave. All the lights should be on by then," Carlos suggested.

"Sounds good," Clay said. "Maybe we can get dessert over there."

"I'm sure there's a large selection of sweets. Wouldn't be an amusement park without it."

"Good point," Clay agreed. "So how are your paintings coming, and when do I get to see them?"

"You want to see them?"

"Of course I do. Why wouldn't I?"

"I thought maybe it wasn't your thing. You haven't mentioned it again since that first day."

"You give me an invite up to your condo. I'd love to see them," Clay said as he reached over and took hold of Carlos's hand once again. "Is this okay?"

"Oh yeah. You can hold my hand anytime you'd like." Okay, now he sounded like a teenage girl on her first date. "I mean, sure it's good."

"You make me laugh," Clay said. "That in itself is a feat."

"I like it when you laugh. All those worry lines disappear."

"What lines? There are no lines on this chiseled face," Clay blustered before sitting back in his chair, but not releasing his hold on Carlos's hand. "I probably had worry lines on my face in utero."

"You didn't get the storybook childhood either?" Carlos asked.

"No, far from it."

"You don't have to tell me anything." Knowing how it felt, Carlos didn't want to force Clay to relive a painful past.

"See, here's the thing... I want to. I haven't wanted to talk about me or my past in a lot of years. But with you, I want to. I want to know everything about you and for you to know me. I know it's intense, but there it is."

"It's not. I want to hear about you."

Clay squeezed his hand before saying, "My mother was a drug addict, and my father was her dealer and pimp, or so they claimed. He could've been a john. I learned at a young age to stay out of the way, to be invisible."

Carlos placed his other hand over the top of their joined hands. "I'm so sorry, Clay. That had to be horrible."

"We aren't so different, you and I. Our prisons may have had different walls, but they were both life-defining. I went into law enforcement while you chose a completely different form of painting than you had been forced to do in the past."

"Too true."

"Hey, I've been wondering why you didn't want Miguel to tell anyone you're his brother."

Carlos leaned back in his chair. "For his protection. He was beginning his military career, and back then, I'd been labeled a criminal for the forgeries. The last thing I wanted was for my legacy to interfere in his climb up his career ladder. I have a feeling you've been looking into me."

"Nothing official. Old newspaper articles and how they accused you of being in on it. A kid. When I read that, I was ready to find the arresting officers and have a word with them."

"It wasn't the officers. They were doing their job. It was the old prosecutor trying to make a name for himself. I know that now. When the guy had a sudden heart attack, a new younger prosecutor was assigned to the case. He figured it out pretty fast, and I was taken out of juvie."

"Thank god," Clay said. "Since you were deemed innocent, why did you have Miguel keep the secret until recently?"

"Did you read about the challenge I faced to prove myself to the art critics?" Carlos asked, hoping that Clay already knew because he didn't want to retell the embarrassing story.

"Yep."

Great. "After that, I buried myself even deeper into isolation and wanted to remain a no one."

"You could never be a no one," Clay countered.

Carlos's heart beat a bit faster at his words. "Time cures all ills, or so they say. I figured things were different now. Miguel is my only remaining family, my brother, and he was getting married. I couldn't stay away. I decided it was time to rejoin the world no matter how painful that may be."

"How is it going so far?"

"Better than I could have ever imagined," Carlos stated, followed by another hand squeeze. "How'd you manage to survive your home life and come out a cop?"

Clay looked down at their joined hands and began rubbing his thumb along the back of Carlos's hand. The intimate gesture wasn't lost on him. "One of my high school teachers took an interest and believed in me. He petitioned the courts to take custody of me after I was arrested at fourteen."

"What were you arrested for?"

"Theft. I took a hotdog from a street vendor. My hunger got the better of me, and I gave in to the impulse. I was put on probation, and Mr. Everett and his wife were awarded temporary custody. They saved my life. No two ways about it. They saw something in me even I hadn't. Mr. Everett was a retired sergeant with the LAPD and inspired me to follow in his path."

"He must have been proud of you. I know I'd be." Carlos thought about how far Clay had come, the battles he must have fought, and the determination it had to have taken to succeed.

"They were by my side the entire way through high school and the police academy. At my graduation, my dad even wore his full-dress uniform in my honor. I don't know what I did to deserve their love and care, but I never took it for granted."

"I'm glad you had the Everetts. Are they still around? Do you see them?" Carlos wondered if he might get to meet them.

"They were already retired when they took me in at fourteen. He taught high school parttime to fill his days. A few years ago, at a ripe old age, they passed away of natural causes within six months of each other. A day doesn't go by that I don't think of them."

Carlos felt warmth spreading inside him. The more he learned about Clay, the more he admired the man. "Did you ever see your biological parents again?" It would be too much to hope they'd cleaned up their act and begged him for forgiveness.

"Yep, once. But neither of them was in any shape to recognize me."

"I'm sorry." That was heartbreaking.

"It's okay. I had the Everetts. They were my mom and dad." Clay's smile was genuine.

"You took their name," Carlos said, having only realized that now.

The smile on Clay's face said it all. "Yep, at eighteen, I decided to change it to theirs legally."

"I bet they were happy," Carlos said as Clay got a faraway look, no doubt remembering the Everetts.

Richard returned with their dinners, and all conversation came to a halt as they dug in. The barbeque sauce was the perfect sticky, smoky, sweet, and tangy covering for the fall-off-the-bone ribs.

Chapter Eight

The flashing lights glowed against the dark sky as they rounded the top of the Ferris wheel for the second time. It took some convincing to get Carlos to get on the ride, but by the smile on his face, Clay felt certain Carlos was having a good time.

"This is the first time I've been on a Ferris wheel," Carlos said as his head whipped from side to side taking everything in. "It's wonderful to see the pier and the beach from a different angle." He took more pictures.

"I'm glad you're enjoying yourself," Clay replied. Considering what Carlos had been through, Clay doubted the guy'd had much fun in his life.

Thanks to the Everetts, Clay had gotten his chance at happiness and fun. Now, he'd give that to Carlos. "How about we drive up the coast next weekend and visit Santa Barbara? It's about a two-hour drive depending on traffic. We could taste some local wines, eat great food, and relax in what's called the American Riviera." The perfect getaway for a man who hasn't seen much of life.

They were halfway to the top again when the Ferris wheel stopped to let people off. Carlos was biting his lip, and Clay wasn't sure if it was because they were hanging in midair or because of his offer.

"Are you okay?"

The big guy turned his handsome face to look at Clay. "Are we dating? Are we monogamous?"

The question caught Clay off guard. He'd never been formally asked before. Most guys knew when they went from flirting to dating, and monogamy was usually a way's off early in a relationship. But this was Carlos, the man who gave people the world in his paintings, but had never seen the world. Clay went with the truth. "I like you, Carlos, and more than simply friendship. I find you funny, interesting, and handsome. When we say goodbye after one of our city tours, I don't want to go, and I'm excited when we have plans. I'd say we're dating if that's all right with you." That was the closest he'd come to romance in what felt like forever, and he hoped it was enough. He'd have to brush up.

The Ferris wheel began moving them up until they were again at the top, and then it stopped.

"Yeah."

"Yeah? You gotta give me a little more than that."

Carlos reached for Clay's hand and said, "I want us to be dating. I feel the same about our time together. I miss you when you're gone."

Clay lifted his free hand to touch Carlos's cheek and leaned in to taste those soft lips that'd held him captivated more than once since meeting the handsome man. At first, the kiss was tentative, slow, a gentle exploration, but within moments need took over, and their tongues dueled as soft moans came up Carlos's throat. As if Clay needed further encouragement, he mapped the inside of his new boyfriend's mouth.

Only when the Ferris wheel began moving again did they break apart, both gasping for air. The kiss had gone from hesitant to raging inferno in a matter of seconds as excitement raced through Clay's blood. His groin was throbbing and he hoped he'd be able to quell the steel in his pants before they got off the ride.

Carlos's cheeks were flushed, and his lips were swollen. He looked gorgeous. Clay turned his head, staring straight ahead to concentrate on getting his wayward cock to calm down. When they reached the bottom, he was reasonably sure he'd gotten himself back under control as they exited the ride.

Once they were away from the crowd, Clay looked over at Carlos to find him staring at the wooden planks of the pier. "What's wrong?"

"I should ask you that," he said. "You kiss me like that, and then you can't bear to look at me. Was it that bad?"

Clay stopped and took hold of Carlos's shoulders to make sure he was looking at Clay. "That kiss blew the doors off my self-control. I had to look away, or I wouldn't've been able to talk myself out of my hard-on before we left our seats."

Carlos's eyes got wide. "Really?"

Instead of answering, Clay pushed him against the nearby wall and took control of Carlos's lips until he had the big man moaning again. The pleasure Clay felt from leaning his overheated body against Carlos's hard frame tested Clay's ability to slow down, but he eventually managed to pull back.

"That's the part of our first kiss I want you to remember. Never any doubts." Clay's voice came out as a growl.

Carlos licked his lips as if chasing a stray taste of Clay. Could Carlos get any sexier? Clay was laser-focused on those wet lips when they turned up into a brilliant smile.

"I'll never forget," Carlos swore as the hanging lights sparkled in his eyes.

"Good. Now let's go win you a stuffed animal," Clay said before taking Carlos's hand and leading him in the direction of the games.

***

A half hour later, Carlos threw his last beanbag at the three stacked blocks to knock them off the pedestal, but once again, one remained on top. As it turned out, they both sucked at midway games. They'd tried their luck at mini hoops, whack-a-mole, ring toss, and now they could add the Beach Dash to that list.

He should be frustrated or disappointed, but Carlos was neither. He was having the best time of his life. Their laughter had been infectious on more than one occasion as other people playing alongside them joined in. Carlos hadn't once been bothered by his anxiety the entire evening and it felt liberating.

"Okay, one last game," Clay said as he pointed across the way. "The Route Sixty-Six Racer."

"I love everything Route Sixty-Six." Carlos grinned at the mere name. "I always dreamed of driving the route. Imagining the freedom was enticing and kept me going at times."

"Well, then maybe this will be the lucky one," Clay said as they made their way over to the little Airstream camper that housed the game.

"Prize or no prize, this has been a great night," Carlos stated.

Clay looked at him with a big smile. "That's what we tour guides like to hear."

They played a classic horse racing game but with hotrods. The players used a water gun to hit the target, and the better your aim, the faster the car moved. Pretty simple, and it even had little cut-out landmarks like the Cadillac Ranch along the way.

Once they'd paid, both took positions side by side and lined up their water guns. When the bell sounded and the water sprayed out, Carlos struggled to keep the stream on the small target. He looked up to see Clay's car taking the early lead out of the five people playing. Carlos was so excited that they might win that he didn't care that his car was dead last.

"Go, go, go," he cheered, making Clay smile.

Moments later, the winning bell sounded, and Clay jumped into the air raising his arms in a mock victory dance that any NFL-er would've been proud to perform.

"Finally, the gods of midway games have taken pity on me." Clay laughed. "Pick which one you like, sweetheart."

Carlos looked between the giant yellow pineapple, raccoons, and what looked like a pug. He noticed a small girl staring at the large Miss Kitty dangling from the top of the camper's overhang, while her mother searched through her purse.

"Go ahead," Clay said, and Carlos didn't hesitate.

"I'll take the kitty," he said while pointing up at the oversized cat head.

The moment it was placed in his hands, Carlos knew where it belonged. Clay followed him over to the girl and her mother. He hoped he'd made the right choice and didn't scare them.

"Excuse me," Carlos said, and when the woman looked up, he saw her eyes go wide. He had expected that reaction. A woman alone with a child had to be wary of strangers. The fact that he towered over her didn't help.

She placed her hand protectively on her daughter's shoulder. "Yes?"

"My boyfriend just won this game over here, and we thought that perhaps your daughter would give this plushie a good home."

The woman looked between them, making Carlos wonder if she had a problem with the LGBTQ community.

The little girl was nearly bouncing with excitement, and Carlos felt a lot better when the mom cracked a smile. "That's very kind of both of you. I'm afraid we haven't had much luck tonight. We're here on vacation, and it certainly is a beautiful place, but I stink at carnie games."

"Until now, we did too. Consider your luck officially changed," Clay said as he moved alongside Carlos and wrapped his arm around him. "This man seems to have that effect on people."

Carlos could feel his face warming and handed the prize over to the girl who promptly wrapped her chubby little arms around it.

"Thank you," the mother said. "Lucy, what do you say to the nice gentlemen?"

The happy little girl looked up at them and in a small voice she said, "Thank you for my kitty."

"You're welcome, Lucy," they said in unison, and then went their separate ways. That moment would surely stick with Carlos always.

"Have you had enough fun for one evening?" Clay asked while pulling him closer.

"Never, but you have an early shift tomorrow, and you should be rested. Besides, I have at least one more painting I'd like to complete before our trip to Santa Barbara."

"When do I get to see them?"

"Soon," Carlos answered. "I want to have a range to show you first."

"Okay. Anytime you're ready, I'll be there." Clay led them away from the game.

Carlos was working on saying something romantic, but his mind went blank, and was replaced by terror as he stared down the last person he ever expected to see again. His former foster father, Earl Roy. He wasn't certain, and he stopped walking. He was now rooted to the wooden planks of the pier, and he was sure.

"Carlos?" Clay's tone was filled with concern. "What's wrong?"

"He's here." Carlos hated that his voice cracked.

Clay scanned the area before asking, "Who?"

"Earl." Carlos didn't even have to explain. Clay knew who Carlos was talking about. "He's standing in front of the Seaside Swing in a green t-shirt and red ball cap." Though his hair was grey and his former boxy face was replaced by sagging skin, Carlos would know those cold, malevolent eyes anywhere.

Clay looked again. "I see him. What do you want to do? I've got your back."

"Thanks," Carlos said. Knowing that Clay was by his side meant the world to him. "I think we should leave and find out why he's not rotting in jail."

"You got it." Clay twined his fingers with Carlos's and led him to the nearest exit.

Carlos didn't know where they were going, but he trusted Clay to get him out of there. He kept glancing back to make sure Earl wasn't following them, but every so often, Carlos would get a glimpse of that green shirt. Was he stalking them? It was more than happenstance that Earl was at the pier. He must've been watching them all along before making his appearance. Shit. Now Clay was in danger.

A couple of quick turns and a set of stairs later, they were back at Clay's car and jumping in. Carlos hadn't seen his foster father since they left the pier, but that didn't mean anything. The bastard had a knack for popping up when he wasn't expected. Point proved by today's appearance. Soon they were on the street and were headed toward DTLA.

"How you doing?" Clay asked as he squeezed Carlos's thigh in reassurance. "You're safe. I'll make sure of it, sweetheart."

"I like it when you call me that," Carlos muttered. His frazzled mind decided to latch onto a piece of romance at that moment.

"Then I'll use it more often," Clay stated. "Your brother's going to meet us back at The Gates."

"When did you have time to call him?" Carlos must have been totally zoned to've missed that.

"On our walk back, I shot off a text when we were waiting for the light to change. You had your eye out for Earl," Clay explained.

"Great. Now I'm about to hear a list of rules he's gonna lay down. My brother's going to go into combat mode." Carlos could already hear Miguel dictating what the game plan would be. Carlos loved his brother, but he tended to be past overprotective. He lived in a guerilla warfare zone when it came to the people he loved.

"Yeah, well, here's the first rule. You're not to leave my side until we get a handle on this situation and discover what the hell he wants," Clay stated.

Staying by his side would be no hardship for Carlos. "Revenge comes to mind. I destroyed Earl's lucrative business and sent him to prison."

"Yeah, built on the back of a child. The bastard should still be rotting in jail for that. Besides, it was the social worker who blew the whistle. You were the victim in all of this."

"I wonder how he's out early?" A heads-up would have been appreciated, instead of this not-so-random meeting.

"We'll find out soon enough, and then we'll deal with it together."

"Are you sure you want to get involved in this?" Carlos asked. He didn't want to drag Clay into whatever mess Earl was about to create, though the thought of facing it alone turned Carlos's stomach.

"I'm positive I want to get involved with you no matter what that means," Clay said. "And this shit with Earl Roy... I'm not going anywhere, sweetheart."

Carlos threaded their fingers together, amazed that he didn't have to face things alone anymore. Between Clay, Miguel, and all his new friends, Carlos had the support he'd longed for and would never take for granted.

***

When they pulled into the back parking lot of The Gates, there was a small battalion waiting for them: Miguel, Finn, Sam, and Max, with Saint and Joey standing in the doorway leading into the back storage area to the restaurant.

Clay was trying his damnedest to keep his anger in check, but the thought of Earl getting anywhere near Carlos was making him see red. Rationally, he understood Carlos wasn't a helpless boy anymore and could defend himself. Still, Clay couldn't fight the need to protect him.

"Stay put. I'll open your door for you," Clay said.

"I'm sure Earl couldn't have made it this far without us seeing him, but I'm good with waiting." Carlos undid his seatbelt.

Clay got out and rounded the front of the car. As he did, he scanned the area before he approached the passenger door. He couldn't be too careful even though Carlos was right. Earl couldn't have made it this far ahead of them. Plus, it wasn't likely he knew where Carlos was living. But how did he know they'd be at the pier? Clay didn't believe in coincidences.

The expression on Miguel's face matched Clay's sentiments exactly, but neither said a word. When Carlos stepped out, his brother was quick to lead him into the protection of The Gates. Clay shut the car door and followed while still keeping an eye out for anything out of the ordinary. Sam, his partner, was doing the same by his side.

"The asshole's out of jail, huh?" Sam asked.

"It would appear that way," Clay answered.

"Did you see him?"

"Yep. I saw the man Carlos said was his former foster father. I've never seen a picture of him before, but I'm positive if Carlos says it was him, it was him." There was no way Carlos would make that kind of mistake.

"Good enough for me. I'd like you to take a look at some recent mugshots to confirm his identity. Then we can open a case on possible stalking charges and put the bastard back where he belongs."

"Sounds like a plan," Clay agreed. "Did you find out how he got out of prison early?"

"Ross is working on that now," Sam assured him.

Ross was a detective with the LAPD, a friend, and Joey's brother James's boyfriend. Seriously, these webs of attachment were getting confusing, and now Clay was jumping into the fray.

They gathered in the hub, the living room area in the temporary living space located in the back of The Gates. It housed Saint, Max, and Marian until the rest of the building was restored. Marian ran the kitchen and behaved like a surrogate mother to anyone who walked through the doors. She was currently using the kitchenette to make coffee for the assembled group.

The moment Carlos saw Clay, he came over and took his hand, catching the attention of the group. Clay could feel a slight tremor work its way down Carlos's arm.

"You wanna sit down?" Clay asked. After all these years, it had to've been a shock seeing the man responsible for so much pain.

"Yeah. It's all hitting me now with the adrenaline crash."

Clay led Carlos over to one of the big armchairs. As he sat, Clay took up a position at his side, never once relinquishing his hold on Carlos's hand. He didn't care what anyone thought or said.

Miguel looked shocked and ready to open his mouth, but Finn brought him in check with a sidelong glance that spoke volumes. Finn was a good guy and didn't take anyone's shit. Along with managing the restaurant and bar, he fed the homeless one day a week from the food he'd collected from local restaurants and businesses. Clay had been homeless as a kid when his parents had spent the rent money on drugs. He appreciated what a gift it was to have people like Finn out there.

"So, who wants to start?" Miguel said while motioning between Clay and Carlos with an accusing finger.

"Do you mean tonight with Earl or this?" Carlos asked as he raised their joined hands. Clay was impressed by his confidence. Miguel could be intimidating.

"Both," Miguel huffed, and Finn punched him in the arm. "What? He's my brother." Finn scowled.

"This." Carlos raised their hands again. "Is me holding my boyfriend's hand, end of discussion. Now, back to the important reason we're all here. Earl Roy was standing about fifty yards away from us when we finished playing a game on the pier."

"You went to Pacific Park?" Miguel asked.

"Yeah, man. I'm not a child. We had dinner first, and the ribs at Del Frisco's Grille are excellent." Carlos gave his brother a challenging glare.

"Oh, I've been there. The ribs are great," Joey agreed as he pressed himself into Sam's side.

Clay watched as Miguel's left eye began to twitch, and wondered how much more off-topic conversation he could take. The next few sentences would prove to be enough.

"Which games did you play?" Marian asked as she joined them with a tray full of cups of coffee. "I used to win every time on that bean bag tossing game."

"What the hell? Am I the only one taking this seriously?" Miguel asked as he looked at everyone.

"Don't get worked up," Carlos said, his voice hard. "I'm taking this seriously, but I refuse to let Earl take away any more of my happiness. Yeah, I saw him. He may've aged twenty years, but it was him."

Sam showed his cell phone to Carlos and then Clay. On it was a picture of Earl Roy.

"Yep, that's the guy we saw," Clay answered. "The asshole was staring straight at Carlos."

"This was taken before his release," Sam said. "Ross sent over the information he's found. It appears Earl Roy was released from Ironwood State Prison a month ago in part due to his good behavior, which made it easier to let him out due to overcrowding. Patricia Roy, though, is still sitting in Central California Women's prison."

"What are the terms of his parole, and who's his parole officer?" Miguel asked like a general demanding intel.

"There are multiple terms he has to adhere to as conditions of his release. The basics are curfew, halfway house, no firearms, and— here it is. He's not to come within one hundred yards of Carlos Fernandez."

"That's where we'll get him," Clay stated. "Next time we'll get the jerk on tape so he can take a one-way trip back to prison. The bastard should have never been let out."

"We'll make a report in the morning and begin gathering evidence. The captain will meet us at the station to get the particulars," Sam explained while shoving his phone back in his pocket and wrapping his arm around Joey.

"Good," Clay stated. "The sooner Roy's back behind bars, the happier we'll all be. I'll sleep on your couch tonight, Carlos."

"What?" Miguel growled. "Why?" His arms were spread wide as if he'd never heard of such a thing.

"To watch over Carlos. I'd think that was obvious." Clay wasn't going to take any of this protective bullshit from Miguel. "You know, we're not talking about a fifteen-year-old hanging out with a thirty-three-year-old. He's a grown-ass man." While Clay appreciated Miguel's position, Carlos didn't need to be shrouded in a virginal blanket.

"This place is like Fort Knox." Miguel wasn't letting it go. "No one is getting in here."

"Clay stays," Carlos cut in. "I love you, brother, but you need to understand this is my life. A life I've fought to have, and I think I deserve. I'm not turning back. Of course, I want you by my side, but I also want Clay, and you need to accept that. You've never had a problem with him before we started dating."

The group had gone mute and silence reigned. Gazes shifted back and forth between the brothers, waiting for the next move.

"That's because he wasn't trying to fuck my brother," Miguel growled. "By his own admission, Clay hasn't had a serious relationship in years. I don't want to see my *brother* get hurt when he," Miguel pointed at Clay, "takes off."

Clay couldn't stop the growl from escaping his lips. While he hadn't been serious with anyone in years, none of this was any of Miguel's business. "No, I haven't. A relationship was the last thing I wanted after being left standing at the altar." Clay turned to Carlos. "Now isn't the time or place I wanted you to hear this. I would've preferred to tell you in private. But if your pain in the fuckin' ass brother needs the truth so bad, he can have it." Clay hated that this shit had to come out in front of an audience.

"I know you would've," Carlos said, then eyed his brother. "I would've too." Miguel glared, not looking the least bit contrite. "You were engaged?" Carlos asked Clay.

"Yep. Over ten years ago. It wasn't meant to be," Clay stated, trying not to get into too many painful details. "But you make me want to take a chance again on a relationship. As for tonight, I refuse to leave you in any possible danger."

"That sucks," Joey said as he hugged his boyfriend, Sam. "I'm sorry you had to go through that."

Carlos pulled Clay closer, making him feel like they were together, together. Warmth spread through him, thawing places long frozen over.

"Fine," Miguel grumbled. "We regroup in the morning. It's getting late, and nothing more can be done tonight."

Carlos stood. "I really need to get some rest," and pulled Clay out of the hub and toward the elevators. "I'm done with peopling for today."

"Whatever you need, sweetheart." Clay would make sure it happened. The amount of strength Carlos had already shown in the face of what had to be horrible memories made what he felt for the handsome man stronger.

Chapter Nine

Carlos woke to a smell so heavenly his mouth began to water in anticipation. Bacon. Was there anything that smelled so good? He pulled on his shorts and headed for the kitchen where he found Clay in his boxer briefs at the stove, moving wooden tongs in a frying pan. Carlos's heart skipped several beats. His boyfriend was making breakfast for him.

Clay's broad shoulders and muscled back tapered into a "V" and those sexy dimples above his firm, muscled butt cheeks were evident above the briefs' waistband. Holy shit, Clay was hot. Carlos liked this look.

Last night, they'd stayed up for a few more hours, talking about what'd happened in the hub, what'd happened on the pier and how that'd brought up shit Carlos didn't want to revisit. Clay had shared his dream of becoming a detective, and Carlos felt they'd turned an important corner—they were really starting something.

"You going to stand there and stare at my ass all day?" Clay asked, bringing Carlos out of his musings. "I'm not complaining, mind you, but the bacon might burn."

"Don't burn the bacon," Carlos ordered. "Though your ass is spectacular."

A red flush worked its way up Clay's throat until it reached his face. "Thanks."

"You're welcome," Carlos chuckled. "So, you can cook?"

"Yep." Clay plucked three eggs from the carton and began juggling them. "Didn't think a cop could cook?"

"No, it's not that. I'm happy one of us can," Carlos replied while watching the sideshow. "Is that a new way of scrambling them that I don't know about?"

Clay caught all three and laughed. "Smartass. How do you want your eggs prepared?"

"Over easy, please. I'll get started on the toast. I can help with the anyone-can-do-this basics."

Carlos joined Clay at the counter, and before he could even reach for the bread, Clay pulled him into his arms. "G'morning."

"'Morning." Carlos lowered his head, seeking a kiss, which his boyfriend quickly gave. "I thought bacon was the best way to start the day, but I was wrong. Your kiss is."

Clay's smile was brilliant. "I vote we try again to make sure." Which they did spectacularly.

After his head stopped spinning, Carlos placed two pieces of bread into the toaster and took out the butter while Clay fried six eggs. It all felt so wonderfully domestic as they worked together until they had two heaping plates sitting on the island's countertop.

Carlos refilled each of their coffee cups before they dug into their morning feast. Carlos could get used to help with food prep as long as Clay was the chef. Not much was said while they ate, neither leaving a crumb over.

"That was delicious." Carlos wiped his mouth, leaned over and gave Clay a quick kiss. "Thanks."

Clay laid his arm along the back of Carlos's chair and said, "You're welcome."

"How was sleeping on the couch?" Carlos had wanted Clay to stay with him in his bed, but he hadn't worked up the nerve to ask. "Not too bad, I hope."

"Not at all. You have a comfortable couch. I slept like a log."

Somehow, Carlos doubted that. Clay had to've been curled up in a ball for his whole body to fit on the sofa. That was enough to convince him to ask. "Why don't you stay with me tonight?"

Clay didn't take any time to answer. "I will. I'd prefer to lay with you in my arms."

Carlos was drawn into another kiss that made him melt into the feel of Clay's soft lips commanding his own. His tongue plunged into Carlos's mouth, drawing out his desire until they were both moaning.

Clay explored Carlos's chest with his warm, rough hands pulling him even deeper under his spell. His fingertips circled Carlos's nipples until they were hard nubs before pinching them hard enough to make Carlos whine with need.

"God, the sounds you make drive me crazy," Clay growled into Carlos's neck, and then dove in for another all-encompassing kiss, which would've brought Carlos to his knees if they hadn't come up for air when they did.

He was moments away from standing and pressing his overheated body into Clay's when a loud banging sounded at the front door. *Shit.*

Clay's annoyed growl said it all. "Seems our time alone has come to an end. We'd better go put on some clothes. It's likely part of the crew or all of them. I'm surprised they waited this long."

"Finn must have hidden my brother's cell phone so he couldn't call at O-dark-hundred," Carlos joked.

"Remind me to thank him." Clay laughed as he dove in for one final kiss before heading to his gym bag on the floor beside the couch.

On the way, he passed by the shut door to Carlos's studio. Clay had respected Carlos's decision to wait to show him his paintings and hadn't once asked to go in. He barely acknowledged the room once Carlos had explained what was behind the door.

"Hold on a minute," Carlos yelled toward the front door, and whoever was who kept knocking.

Today was going to be a long day.

***

After providing their full statements to Detective Ross, the captain officially assigned Clay to Carlos's protection until they figured out where Earl Roy was hiding. He hadn't returned to his halfway house for curfew the night before, and he was still at large, probably realizing after he was identified and that would be the first place the police looked. The breach of his parole conditions, combined with their statements, should be enough to get Earl back to prison.

The news that the asshole was out there somewhere possibly waiting for Carlos to emerge from The Gates had Clay on edge, but he buried it. He didn't want to worry Carlos, who'd been shut in behind his studio door for the past couple days, only coming out to eat and sleep.

They'd been sharing the same bed since the second night of Clay's moving into the condo, and he was surprised by how easily their new routine came together. There hadn't been any significant compromises or concessions made. From which side of the bed each slept on, to their weird sleeping patterns, they fit. With each passing day, Clay found himself falling deeper and becoming more attached to Carlos. He was feeling emotions long since buried, which he would've thought he'd fear, given his history, but he embraced their intimacies and their conversations.

Clay had made it his mission to search through Earl's prisoner file to gain some knowledge about who the man was and who he'd been in contact with during his incarceration that might be helping him now. So far, he had a list of four people who had visited Earl regularly over the years and had also sent him mail. The captain made it possible for Clay to have remote access to the LAPD database. The captain had agreed having more eyes on this case would be welcomed, and since Carlos had his work, Clay had time on his hands.

The four individuals included a member of a religious charity, Roy's lawyer, a man named Jacob Russell, and a woman named Sally Roy. As Clay dug deeper into Earl Roy's history, Clay was surprised to discover that Earl had divorced his first wife, Patricia, from behind bars and married Sally, who, at this point, was a complete unknown.

Clay shot a text off to Sam even though he felt certain Ross had already caught the new marriage connection, but it never hurt to check. California was one of the last few states that offered conjugal visits for their inmates in state-run facilities, and it appeared Sally had been on that list. Earl had to've put on some stellar behavior to be allowed that particular type of visitation.

Earl had been an inmate at Ironwood, a medium-security prison for the past nineteen years, and seemed to've stayed under the radar. Clay almost spit out his coffee when he read that the man had even become a minister while serving his time. What the hell was going on in there? If Earl had turned over a new leaf, showing up at the pier didn't fit that profile. More likely, he did what he thought would work to get conjugal visits, and to convince the parole board he was an acceptable risk to leave the facility.

"How goes the research?" Carlos asked as he exited his studio. His paint-stained smock was open, revealing his dark, hairy chest and abs, making it impossible for Clay to look away. He itched to run his fingers through that delicious fur.

With more willpower than he thought he had, Clay looked up to find Carlos staring at him with the same burning desire. The memory of breakfast the first morning still ran on repeat in his mind. How good Carlos tasted, and the sounds he made echoed in his ears. Since that morning, by tacit agreement they kept their physical relationship on simmer. The tension of knowing Earl Roy was out there put a damper on exploring what they clearly both wanted. They kissed goodnight, and stayed connected in their sleep, but that's as far as it went. Not to say their bodies didn't broadcast a different message. Both of them had serious wood in the briefs every time they got near each other. Apparently, their bodies had bypassed their reserve and there were no barriers holding them back.

"Yes?" Clay asked, both knowing what he was really asking.

"Hell yes." Carlos smiled and nodded.

Clay was off the couch and across the room in the blink of an eye. He took hold of Carlos's hand and led him to the bedroom. Clay started to unbutton Carlos's painting smock the rest of the way, Clay's hands brushing against his man's hard abdominal muscles. A soft growl worked its way up Clay's throat as he slid the piece of fabric away from Carlos's body. "Damn, sweetheart. You make a man want."

Carlos dove in with a kiss filled with passion and need, confirming they were on the same page, and neither could wait any longer. He took hold of Clay's shirt and pulled, not bothering to undo the buttons, which clattered on the wood floor as Carlos ripped the shirt off Clay's body. Clay had never been so turned on in his life, and he wanted more.

"Up on the bed, sweetheart, so we can get those jeans off you," Clay instructed with a slap to Carlos's firm ass cheek.

Carlos did as Clay asked without question and sat staring at him as if he had all the answers. Complete trust and raw need. Fuck, what a powerful combination. Clay knew he'd never be the same after making love with Carlos, and he didn't fear that reality at all.

Clay jumped onto the bed and straddled his sexy man's thighs before unbuttoning his jeans and slowly lowering the zipper. Deliberately, he brushed his fingers over the hard bulge underneath, eliciting a hiss that was music to his ears. Clay fought the urge to move faster, but slowed down so they could fully enjoy their first time together.

Once he managed to get Carlos down to his boxer briefs, Clay removed his jeans and rejoined him on the bed. Clay took his time, lavishing Carlos's legs with kisses and soft bites as his mouth travelled up from ankle to thigh. Given the big guy's height, the journey took time, and Carlos was writhing by the time Clay reached the edge of Carlos's boxers.

Pressing down on Carlos's hips to try to hold him in place, Clay licked and mouthed his lover's hard cock through the briefs. Every moan and shudder he caused made Clay want to flip Carlos over and possess him, but the tease was too delicious to rush things. As he pulled down Carlos's briefs, he ran his hands through thick, soft hair until he reached taut nipples begging for attention. Clay leaned over and in turn nipped and sucked at each bud until Carlos was groaning.

"Cl—Clay, damn, you're making me crazy. Please, I need to feel you inside of me." Carlos's voice was hoarse and deep.

"All in good time." Clay had more exploration planned before he sank his cock into his man's luscious ass.

Clay made his way down Carlos's torso back to the prize, and took his thick cock in his mouth and sucked that long, juicy treat until he knew Carlos was close. Then Clay backed off and began to lick Carlos's heavy balls while rimming his hole lightly with his finger. When he thought Carlos was about to blow, Clay backed off again and repeated his torture until *he* couldn't take it anymore.

"Sweetheart," Clay's voice was barely a rumble. "Where's your lube and condoms?"

"Top drawer, side table," Carlos grunted as Clay bit down on his right nipple without breaking the skin.

Clay knew what he'd do to make Carlos's orgasm slam hard. There were so many things he wanted to do to this addictive man. Clay had to remind himself they had time to explore. Clay intended for the two of them to be together going strong for a long, long time.

***

Carlos had never experienced most of the sensations he was feeling. His former fuck buddy wasn't in the same league as Clay. Carlos couldn't help hissing when Clay removed his boxers, causing his cock to slap against his stomach. Turned on beyond his wildest imaginings, his body was coiled with need and his cock wept with want.

He was drowning in desire as his body came to life under Clay's sensual attention. His muscled body felt incredible when Clay laid on top of him, and he could hardly wait to feel the full force of the power in Clay's hips.

Carlos watched as his lover stretched to reach the side table and near jumped out of his skin when Clay's cock bounced on top of Carlos's. He needed to feel their bodies connect and was wired waiting for Clay to slide his beautiful cock into him.

Carlos fisted the sheets at the snap of the tube's top. Clay dripped the lube onto the first two fingers of his right hand. Carlos's body was vibrating in anticipation of the pleasures to come.

Clay's cock bobbed in front of Carlos's face as Clay lay beside him, his mouth latched onto Carlos's hip as Clay slid his fingers between Carlos's ass cheeks. The insertion of Clay's lubed fingertip caused a lust-filled moan to escape Carlos's lips. He pulled the bottom half of Clay's body closer so he could wrap his mouth around his lover's hard cock.

The groan vibrating through Clay's chest served to spur Carlos on as he sucked and licked until he felt Clay's legs shaking.

"Two can play at that game, sweetheart," Clay said moments before sliding the second finger into him.

Carlos held on tight to his prize even though he was tempted to throw his head back and roar. He deep-throated Clay's beautiful cock making him buck his hips and drive himself deeper down Carlos's throat. Their pleasure echoed through the room. Nothing existed beyond this bed.

Clay took his time adding a third finger, stretching Carlos while he increased the speed of his bobbing head as he rolled Clay's balls in the palm of his hand. When Clay's finger brushed against Carlos's prostate, he nearly shot off the bed, and from that moment on, Clay continued to peg the sensitive gland with every thrust.

Carlos didn't know how much more he could take before blowing and was about to pull off when Clay removed his fingers and Carlos released Clay's thick cock. He shifted his body, and then handed the condom to Carlos. One last silent request for permission.

Without any doubt, he rolled the latex down Clay's cock and gave him a few pumps for good measure, causing Clay to groan.

"You are playing with fire, sweetheart," Clay growled. His stunning, azure eyes seemed to light from within. "I'm barely hanging onto my control as it is."

"Damn, you're fuckin' sexy," Carlos growled back. "Go for it, man. I can handle those flames."

Clay repositioned himself, stuffed a pillow under Carlos's hips, and slowly slid his lubed cock between Carlos's ass cheeks. Every brush against his needy hole was a tease, and by the grin on Clay's face, it was meant to be.

"Do you want me to beg?" Carlos asked, fully prepared to do it.

"I never want to hear you beg for anything for the rest of your life, sweetheart," Clay replied before lining his cock up with Carlos's hole and sliding in.

The pressure became pleasure when Clay was fully seated inside of him. Gasping from the intense pleasure, Carlos watched his lover's near pained expression. Clay was holding himself still, not only waiting for Carlos's body to become accustomed to the girth, but also for Clay to keep himself from letting it go too soon. When he began to move, Carlos had to close his eyes as Clay clamped his hands on Carlos's ankles, holding him open and in place. When Clay began pistoning his hips, the bump and slide targeted Carlos's prostate again, but this time, there was no holding back.

A fire burned through his veins as a chorus of lewd noises filled the bedroom. Clay leaned forward to run his rough hands across Carlos's chest, leaving trails of goosebumps across his overheated skin, before Clay reached for him, wrapping those calloused hands around Carlos's cock. When he began to pump in time to his thrusts, Carlos pushed up on his arms to meet his lover halfway, desperate to feel his kiss, which was broken by their need to breathe. Everything in that moment centered on them and their joined bodies reaching for release.

Carlos fell back onto the mattress, arms wide, with his fingers buried into the sheets. With every thrust and stroke, Carlos's balls tightened, feeling the tingle hit before electricity shot across his body, down his spine, into his balls, and out the tip of his cock. His orgasm slammed through him, taking away his breath. His heart thudded in his ears and he knew he'd never come this hard.

Clay's loud growl-groan filled the room as he jetted inside Carlos, his cock twitching against the walls of his body. Clay braced himself on his arms above Carlos as they both heaved heavy breaths. Carlos reached up, pulled his smiling lover down on top of him, and wrapped his arms around a strongly muscled back.

Clay stroked Carlos's hair back from his sweaty forehead. "You all right?"

Carlos shrugged. "I guess."

Clay nipped Carlos's lower lip then whispered, "Bastard," before threading his fingers into Carlos's hair and grabbing a fistful, yanking hard enough for Carlos to ride the edge of pain. "I see I'm gonna have to teach you a few lessons."

For the next few hours, Clay made sure Carlos knew who owned his body, and did it spectacularly.

Hours later, exhausted in the best possible way, Clay stroked Carlos's neck, their legs entwined unable to completely break their connection. "Do you want to know how I got the scar?" Carlos asked.

Clay pulled Carlos closer. "Only if you are ready to tell me."

Five months ago, if anyone had told Carlos he'd be ready to share his past with the man he believed was his future, he would've told them to get fucked. Now, he knew he was where he was supposed to be with a man who accepted him for who he was.

"I was about a year out of juvie, and I worked odd jobs in the neighborhood to make extra money. I was coming home from the burger joint, where I'd been paid cash to wash dishes, when I heard a woman scream. It had to be two o'clock in the morning, so I followed her screams to help. I came up to the alley behind a little market and found a man choking a woman who was taking out the trash. The black bags were broken open on the ground behind him."

"Anyway, I rushed up behind the guy and pulled him away from the woman, clocked him, and he fell to the pavement. I leaned down to help the victim get up, and as I was turning around to check on her attacker, the asshole jumped on my back and wrapped a wire around my throat. The woman ran back into the store as we struggled. I could feel the metal digging into my neck, so I slammed him back against the wall to break his hold. I could hear sirens getting closer, but by then I was having a hard time breathing and close to passing out when I heard a single gunshot. The dude went limp and I collapsed."

"When I woke up, I was in the hospital with my neck covered in bandages like a mummy. That's when I found out the woman hadn't run back into the store and abandoned me. She went to get her gun."

"You saved her life, and she repaid the favor. You're a hero," Clay said.

"No hero. Simply a guy in the right place at the right time," Carlos stated. "In the end, the lady saved me."

"Whether you believe you're a hero doesn't change the facts. If you hadn't searched for the source of the screaming, he would've killed her. You gave her a chance to get her weapon. A sad truth, a lot of people would've kept walking."

"Believe me, no one looks at me and thinks hero. I'm the scary big dude with the scar that everyone avoids."

Clay shook Carlos's shoulders. "To me, and that woman, you are a hero. Never doubt that."

Carlos shrugged. Potato, potahto. Perspective was a weird thing. To change the subject and satisfy his curiosity, he asked, "So, you were engaged?"

"Yep. Feels like a lifetime ago," Clay answered. "I was young, stupid, and in love. As it turned out, a toxic combination."

"What happened?" Carlos asked but said quickly, "If you don't want to relive it, I understand."

"No. I don't mind telling you. I had intended to, but the night Miguel forced my hand, the time and place didn't allow for details."

"I'm sorry he's behaving like an overbearing psycho." His brother had lost his mind. Between monitoring the entrances and keeping tabs on Carlos at all times, Miguel was making him nuts. He even went so far as to suggest Carlos wear a tracker around his ankle. Off his fucking mind.

"Miguel loves you and he's trying to protect you, even if he's acting like an ass," Clay said, which surprised him since his brother had been treating Clay like shit on the bottom of his shoe.

"I know, but it's hard not to slip into what's been comfortable for years and hide out. Miguel's behavior intensifies that feeling. I don't want to go back to the way things were."

"I can understand that." Clay nodded.

"Sorry, we got off-topic," Carlos said. "I want to hear about what happened with your fiancé."

"Saying he left me at the altar is the make-you-feel-sorry-for-me response. In actuality, we were meeting at city hall. It wasn't a big affair, only a handful of people. I was excited waiting for his arrival when I got a call letting me know he wasn't showing up. He'd changed his mind."

Talk about a low blow. Carlos noticed Clay didn't say the guy's name when talking about him. "Just like that?"

"Yep. The coward didn't have the balls to face me, so he called. We'd been together since college and I *thought* he'd stood by me through the academy. We'd planned on marrying after I was hired onto the force."

"Did he even give you a reason?"

Clay stared up at the ceiling for a moment before answering.

"After all the hard work and sacrifice, I was finally a police officer, and he decided he couldn't live with a cop. The messed-up hours, no holidays off for a rookie, and the danger were all part of his excuse. It wasn't worth it to him. I wasn't worth it."

Carlos didn't know if Clay meant to say that last sentence aloud. It'd been spoken so softly. There was no way in hell Carlos would allow him to continue thinking that about himself.

"You're worth everything to me," Carlos said. "By the sounds of it, it wasn't your worth but his commitment. Leaving it to the wedding day was cruel. He's not a man worth your time, not the other way around."

Clay turned to look at Carlos. "Deep down, I guess I worry if I'm enough."

He understood that feeling and empathized. "You are more than enough. Talk is cheap without something to back it up." Carlos raised onto his elbow to look down into Clay's troubled face. "So instead, I swear I'll convince you of that by my actions every day we're together until you believe it yourself."

Clay raised his hand and cupped the side of Carlos's face, the gesture sending warmth through his body. "You're a treasure."

Carlos could feel his blush working its way up his neck until his cheeks burned. He was sure his foster parents saw him as a goldmine to be exploited for their gain, but to be treasured was something new.

Clay's hand guided Carlos's face down until their lips met in a tender, almost reverent kiss that showed him better than words ever could how Clay felt.

Carlos would never forget this moment. Ever.

Chapter Ten

Carlos pulled his old duffle bag from the closet and threw it on the bed. Clay had gone to a meeting at the station with Captain Myers, Sam, and Ross. Carlos figured he'd use this time to get some packing done for the upcoming Santa Barbara weekend.

Earl hadn't been found, but Carlos refused to cancel their plans. He'd spent too many years locked inside either by his foster parents or from his self-imposed isolation. The feeling of being trapped lingered below the surface, tweaking his stress and anxiety. He had to get out of his condo before he lost it. Besides, Clay would be right there by his side, and he'd be armed. Having a lover who was a cop had its benefits.

Those endless days locked inside his bedroom where every creak, scrape, and footstep were terrifying was long over, and he'd sooner face Earl than go back to his former existence. Harsh, but now that he'd had a taste of what life could be, he didn't want to tuck tail and run. Not again. He was more than willing to fight for a future with a handsome officer by his side.

Carlos had been wracking his brain, trying to think of anything that might help the police find Earl. Considering he'd spent most of his days locked in his room, he never knew Earl's schedule or who he worked with. It'd been a shock to him to find out Earl had divorced his wife-in-crime. The two had been well suited. From their cruelty to their penchant for violence, they fit.

Clay had been keeping tabs on the investigation and doing some research of his own. He'd gotten Miguel to lay off fucking with Clay, which helped relieve some of Carlos's stress. His brother had gone off the deep end with his protectiveness, and would have stood guard outside the condo door if Finn hadn't dragged him away.

Carlos worried that the closer he got to Clay, he and his brother would drift apart. The thought of losing either of them terrified him.

Fuck. Earl Roy had managed to put a cloud over Carlos's newfound happiness decades after the asshole had been arrested.

Carlos shoved socks and underwear into his bag, followed by shirts, jeans, and a couple of dressier options if they went out to dinner at a nice place. With each item he packed, the more committed he became. He'd never allow Earl Roy to destroy his life again.

His inner ramblings were interrupted when his phone rang. He hoped it was Clay calling to tell him he was on his way back to the condo.

"Hello."

"Carlos, it's Jeremy calling."

"Oh hey, Jeremy," Carlos greeted his manager. "What's up?" They'd talked a few days ago about all the shit going on in his life, and hoped nothing else was wrong.

"I wanted to check in with you to see how you're holding up with everything that's going on in California." His manager sounded concerned and maybe even a little stressed.

"I'm good. Really. This place is giving me plenty of inspiration. I'll have the new series of paintings done in plenty of time for the upcoming show."

"I love your new work. That's not what I'm talking about. I'm more concerned with your mental health. Are you positive coming out into the public eye is the safest move for you with that piece of shit Earl Roy snooping around?"

"Thanks, man, but trust me, I have never felt more alive than I do right now. I'm happy here with my brother and Clay. I think I've finally found my home." He was becoming more certain of that statement with every passing day.

"I'm happy for you, buddy. Stay safe and make sure to invite me to the wedding," Jeremy joked.

"That possibility isn't even on the radar, but if it ever does head in that direction, you'll be on the list." Jeremy had been working for Carlos almost as long as he'd been free.

"Thanks," he said. "Be careful, and I look forward to seeing more from this new series."

"I have a few I finished this week from our trip to Santa Monica, and another is a work in progress. I'll make sure to send pictures off before we leave for the weekend."

"The weekend? I hope your man is whisking you somewhere nice."

"Santa Barbara." Carlos was excited. He'd never been there, and heard it was gorgeous.

"I've stayed at The Biltmore in Santa Barbara once, beautiful place. You have to check out the wharf. Where are you guys staying?"

"We have a reservation at the Hotel Californian. I'm surprising him. I'll mention the wharf, though he's probably thought of it, but I'll doublecheck."

"Well, I look forward to seeing your latest paintings. Have a fun weekend, and try to relax if you can."

"I will," Carlos said. "Thanks, Jeremy." Good of him to check in. Carlos didn't have a frame of reference since he didn't know how other managers worked, but Jeremy had always done right by him, and had become a friend over the years.

***

Clay stared at Captain Meyers, unsure if he'd heard him correctly. "Dead?"

"Yeah. We received the report this morning," Meyers stated. "Earl Roy's body was discovered at four-thirty this morning beside City Honors High School over in Inglewood."

"How'd he die?" Sam asked, seeming as shocked as Clay felt.

"Single gunshot to the head," Meyers answered. "A nine-millimeter Luger was found in his right hand."

"Suicide?" Couldn't be. Clay wasn't ready to buy into that.

"Appears that way, but the investigation is still ongoing," Meyers answered. "I thought you'd be happy about this."

"I am, but I've been reading through Earl Roy's file and he doesn't come across as a man who'd take his own life." Someone else's, sure, but he was too selfish a bastard to take his own.

"Maybe he knew he was headed back to prison and snapped," Sam suggested.

"Possibly. I'll give you that." Clay had to agree there was a chance, however slim.

"Maybe now Miguel won't be eyeing up every person coming into The Gates," Ross said. "Saint will appreciate that."

"So will Carlos," Clay muttered. "He's been trapped inside a large portion of his life, and simply the thought of taking more of his freedom away wasn't sitting well with me."

"Aren't you two supposed to be headed to Santa Barbara this weekend?" Sam asked.

"Yep. We're leaving tomorrow morning." Not soon enough.

"When you return, I'll have to bring you back from special assignment now that the risk to Carlos is gone," Captain Meyers explained.

That worried Clay, but he understood. The absence of a threat means no need for a police presence.

"I'll report back here Monday morning," Clay reluctantly agreed.

"If we discover anything further regarding Earl Roy, I'll make sure you and Carlos are notified," the captain assured Clay.

The captain was a straight-up guy. He'd never risk someone if there was a chance he could stop it. Knowing that didn't help calm Clay's nerves about Carlos losing police protection. *His protection.* Clay wasn't buying into the death being a suicide. Earl Roy was an egotistical narcissist and was only concerned about himself and how to further his own needs and wants. A man like that wouldn't turn a gun on himself. Who did was the million-dollar question.

"Has there been anything found out about the other people on Earl's visitor list?" Clay asked.

"A representative for the charity stated that they haven't spoken to Earl Roy in over three months. Sally Roy moved to Medford, Oregon a couple of months ago, and we have no reason to believe she's been back to this area since. Jacob Russell is serving ten to twenty in Avenal State Prison for being the wheelman in a robbery down in San Clemente."

"Well, that puts a tidy bow on everything, doesn't it? I'm always suspicious of anything that resolves itself so neatly," Detective Ross said. "Call me cynical." The man was a top detective with the LAPD and had years of experience to draw on. When he made an observation, people listened.

Clay agreed with Ross, but hoped for Carlos's sake the whole business was truly over. The stress radiating from him the last couple of days was a tangible thing, and no matter what Clay had done to take his mind off it, and he'd been very creative, it didn't seem to last.

"If there's nothing further, Captain, I'd like to head back to The Gates." Now that Clay would be returning to patrol, he felt as if he and Carlos needed to spend as much time together as they could.

"Yeah, that's about all of the new information we have now," the captain answered. "Try to enjoy your weekend."

Clay was up and out of his chair before the last word was spoken. He had someone waiting for him "at home." This would be one of the last times he'd be able to say that. With the threat over, Clay would have to return to his apartment. The thought of it made him quicken his pace as he headed to his car. If this would be the last few days they had living together, then he intended to make the most of every moment.

***

When he reached The Gates, Clay stopped by Saint's office to give him an update so the entire crew could stand down. He knocked on the office door, and Saint's voice hollered for him to come in.

The office was unusually busy for the middle of the morning. Saint, Max, Miguel, and Finn sat at various desks. Saint looked to be going through the mail, while Miguel and Max flipped through architectural drawings, and Finn worked on his laptop.

"Clay," Saint called. "How'd your meeting go? Any news?"

"Yep. Earl Roy's body was discovered this morning with a bullet wound to the side of his head."

Miguel stood and came over to him, where he stood a few feet from Saint's desk. "He's dead?"

"There's still an ongoing investigation, but the captain has been told it was suicide. Allegedly, Earl snapped when he realized he'd be going back to prison."

"Really?" Finn asked. "That's wonderful... I mean, it's not great that the dude is dead and all, but Carlos is safe now."

"Not so fast," Miguel said. "What if he was working with someone?"

"That's what I thought, but all his visitors from the prison log have been accounted for."

"So it's over?" Saint asked.

"Until the investigation into Roy's death is closed, it's an ongoing case. But, I'm being recalled to the station Monday because they believe the threat is over." Clay hoped they were right.

"Hallelujah," Max cheered. "Guess you guys are off to Santa Barbara. The two of you can relax now and enjoy yourselves."

"Yep. We leave in the morning." Clay would still keep his guard up just in case.

"You're still going?" Miguel looked at him like he grew another head.

"Of course we are." Why wouldn't they be?

"I don't think that's a wise decision, at least not until they confirm Earl Roy committed suicide." Miguel's facial expression read, *I dare you to disagree.*

As one to always rise to the challenge, Clay said, "Carlos has been forced to stay inside most of his life. I won't do that to him again. Earl Roy is dead and I'll be right by Carlos's side the entire time we're away." He felt like he was seventeen and was talking to Carlos's dad.

"It's too dangerous," Miguel growled. "He can't leave."

Clay was about to lay into Miguel. He was good and tired of his 'tude, but Clay didn't get the chance.

"I *can't* leave!" Carlos's voice was cold and hard, his face like stone.

Shit.

Chapter Eleven

Carlos could feel his anger rising like a wave. His brother was okay with locking him up. Again. Miguel said he loved him, and Carlos knew he did, but Miguel was acting like Earl Roy by confining him to the building.

"It's not safe," Miguel said before crossing his arms over his chest with an *I'm done talking about it* expression. A position he often took when they spoke about this subject. Carlos knew a wall when he saw one.

"Earl is dead. I'm finally free of him." Carlos knew he sounded callous being happy about someone's death, even Earl's, but Carlos couldn't deny his relief.

"He could have been working with someone," Miguel argued. "That person might still be out there waiting for a chance at you. I'm better prepared for situations like this than you are. I know what could happen."

"What would this unknown someone gain?" Carlos asked, his voice rising in exasperation. "Earl's incentive was revenge, but to anyone else, I'm no one."

"Don't say that," Clay growled.

Carlos couldn't help but smile at his boyfriend. The man always took his side even against himself. Carlos wasn't trying to cause anyone to worry, but where would this end? With him back at the beginning where he'd started, in solitude, if Miguel had his way.

"It doesn't matter," Miguel huffed. "It's too dangerous to leave the building."

That was the last straw. Carlos couldn't take any more of Miguel's bullshit. "What the hell is wrong with you? You're acting crazy."

"There's nothing wrong with me," Miguel argued. "Can't you see I want to keep you safe?"

"I am safe." Carlos pointed at Clay. "Cop. By. My. Side." Clay grinned. "Even if I weren't, this is my shot at living free. I need to push forward. I can't go back to the way things were."

"So you'll stand out in the open and wait for someone to take that shot." Miguel jammed his fists into his hips. "You care so little for this new life you keep talking about that you're willing to throw it away so easily?"

"Who's going to take a shot at me? You're not making sense. Please tell me what's going on in that brain of yours. Help me understand." Carlos didn't want to argue with his brother. He loved Miguel.

Their voices rose with the back and forth, and Carlos's anger was making him shake, but he wouldn't back down. He'd fought too hard to get where he was now, and there was no way anyone would stop him. Not even his brother.

"I'm making complete sense," Miguel argued. "I might not have been able to save my parents, but I'll be damned if I lose my brother."

Carlos took a step back as if the truth forced him to. He'd been looking at this from his own perspective and hadn't considered what Miguel had lost. His father and their mother had died in a car accident while Miguel was away on duty, stationed in another part of the world. Not only couldn't he prevent it from happening, he wasn't there to grieve over their graves.

Now that Carlos was in danger, those old fears and regrets must've come back, taking over the rational side of Miguel's brain. Carlos's heart ached for his brother, and all the anger drained from his body.

"You're not going to lose me," Carlos said in a calmer tone of voice. "Accidents are out of anyone's control. There's nothing you could have done to save them whether or not you were in the country. It's not your fault they died." Carlos's eyes began to sting as he tried his damnedest to fight off the tears that threatened. His brother was in pain, and instead, Carlos had been consumed with his own needs. He hadn't stopped to realize the toll this was taking on Miguel. "I'm sorry." Carlos's voice broke as he spoke. "I should've taken them into consideration."

He crossed the room and took his brother into his arms. Miguel didn't fight him and hugged him back. Moments later, Carlos heard the office door closing, and when he glanced around, they were alone. The rest of the crew had left to give them their privacy.

"Why didn't you tell me how you were feeling from the start?" That information certainly would have curbed most of their arguments.

Miguel sat down on one of the office chairs, leaned over, and buried his face in his hands. "I'm sorry I've been acting like an overbearing asshole. I can't seem to stop myself. Every time you're out of my sight, all I can think about is what if I never see you again. What if that was the last time we spoke, the last time forever. I'd rather have you angry with me than dead."

Carlos rolled another chair over and sat facing his brother. "Life is full of danger. You of all people know that well enough, but we can't stop living it. I tried. I locked myself away. I didn't need Earl Roy to set the lock. I did it to myself for decades."

Miguel looked up and Carlos saw the anguish his brother had been hiding for over a week. "It's hard to let go of the past. Always thinking that somehow I had failed to protect them. That their deaths were my fault. I should've been here taking care of them instead of patrolling some arbitrary line in the sand a world away."

"None of what happened was your fault. You answered the call to serve our country. What you did was heroic. Never downplay that for any reason. Not everyone has the bravery you needed to carry out your duty. Your dad and our mom must have been so proud of you. I know I am." Then it hit Carlos what he had to do. "I won't go to Santa Barbara. I'll stay here until you're confident the danger has passed."

Miguel's head shot up, and he seemed to be searching Carlos's face for something. He wasn't sure what, but Miguel must have found it. "You'd do that for me?"

"Of course, I would. You're my brother and I love you. Now that I understand where you're coming from, I don't want you to suffer and worry if I can help it. Clay'll understand."

"So, yeah, that guy. You sure about that?" Miguel's eyebrows drew together.

"Positive." Carlos couldn't help the smile that broke over his face.

"He treats you well?"

"The best. Clay makes me dream of more. I never did that before now." The future had always been a black void with nothing to look forward to. Bleak and desolate except for his art. Now that'd changed along with his new life, and there was no turning back.

"Okay, cause if he ever fucks you over, I'll rip off his dick."

"Don't do that. I'm rather fond of it."

Miguel covered his ears. "I don't want to know what my brother does in the bedroom. Keep that shit to yourself." By the smile on his face and his demeanor, Carlos could tell he was joking.

"I love you, Miguel. You're my brother. I don't want to argue anymore."

"Neither do I. You're right. He's a cop. You'll be safe. You and Clay should go to Santa Barbara."

That change in positions almost gave Carlos whiplash. "Okaaay."

"Earl Roy is dead. Who knows, he may've eaten a bullet, or it could have been a drug deal gone wrong, a robbery, a dispute with a pimp, who knows. The point is any number of people could have done the job, and it has nothing to do with you or your past. Don't get me wrong. I'll still be looking out for you for the rest of your life, but I suppose Clay can take on some of the duty."

"And I'll be looking out for you. That's what brothers are for," Carlos said. "I want you in my life."

"Just not the insanely overprotective me," Miguel said with a grin.

"Even him. But, if there is a next time—and I hope to hell there isn't—tell me what's going on so I can understand. Had I known what you were going through, I would have never pushed so hard."

"Deal. Better communication. Got it." Miguel stood, and Carlos followed. "You two have a good time. Find lots of...inspiration."

"Will do," Carlos agreed, amazed at how much lighter he felt now that the pressure had lifted.

He couldn't wait to hit the PCH with Clay and leave all the trouble of this past week far behind. Their adventure would take them north along the PCH to the Pleasant Valley exit, where they'd connect to the 101 to continue on to Santa Barbara. The whole plan excited Carlos and he was ready to dive in.

***

The next morning Clay set their luggage by the front door for their two-night getaway. Carlos had been in his studio for over thirty minutes, and Clay wondered if he should make more coffee in case they were here longer than expected. His man loved the java.

If a creative urge hit, Clay understood and respected that plans could change. He was on his way back to the kitchen to set up the coffee machine when he heard the studio door open.

"Clay," Carlos called out.

Changing directions at the last moment, he continued into the living room to find Carlos waiting for him with the door to his studio standing wide open.

"What's up?" He didn't want to make any assumptions even though he hoped for a peek at Carlos's paintings. "Everything okay?"

"Yeah," Carlos said with a big smile. "I want to share a few of my recent paintings with you, and a single older one."

"If you're ready, I'm all for it," Clay said. "I'd love to see what you came up with from the trips we took." He'd made a conscious effort not to look or ask about the studio until Carlos was ready.

Carlos held out his hand. "Yeah. I'm ready to share everything about me with you."

Clay took hold of the offered hand and followed Carlos into his studio. The first thing he noticed was the variety of lighting in the room. From the large window, floor-level lamps, overhead bulbs that looked like daylight lighting, and a lot of lamps stationed around the room.

"Tell me what you feel and see," Carlos said as he gestured to the back of the room.

Lined up on a table leaning against the far wall were seven paintings, with the one on the end still covered by a piece of fabric. Carlos ushered him forward, and as he neared the table, Clay saw the first painting was of him. He was sitting in the garden in Little Tokyo with his elbows on his knees, hands joined, and head down. Even with no discernable facial features, he knew it was him. Clay remembered Carlos taking the picture but never thought it would be for him to create a painting.

What had he been thinking about when Carlos took those snaps? Clay searched his memory and realized he'd been trying to hide his emotions. He hadn't wanted to scare off the big guy as he was coming out of his shell, and Clay wasn't sure he wanted more than a fuck after years of protecting his heart. From the bend of his neck, and the coloration of the painting, he looked contemplative as he stared at one of the stone lanterns set in the stream. There were so many emotions loaded into this one scene: worry, confusion, and a sense of longing. *Shit, Carlos had been right.*

"Is this what you meant when you approached me at the wedding? When you said I was longing for something."

Carlos came up beside him. "Yeah."

Clay wrapped his arm around Carlos's waist. "I see it now."

"What were you thinking there?" Carlos asked.

"That I had to quell my desire to be near you."

"Now that I know what happened with the engagement, I understand why you fought it as hard as you did. It's difficult to risk it all again."

Clay took a deep breath and moved on to the next painting. This one depicted the downtown traffic that first day Carlos had gone out to take pictures. It grabbed his attention right away and laid bare the different stages of the Hollywood dream, from elation to disillusionment. The third showcased an older man selling trinkets outside a local store in Little Tokyo. Instead of feeling sad, as Clay had thought it would make him, the painting highlighted perseverance and strength in the face of strangers ignoring the salesman. His slight grin and upturned face toward the sun almost lit the old man from within.

The fourth was of The Gates, the bar specifically, highlighting the wood carvings, showcasing the sweeping staircase. The angelic carving seemed to glow above the bar-top filled with people in various poses as the world streamed outside the tall front windows.

"That one won't be sold," Carlos said. "It'll be in the showing, but it belongs to Saint."

Having heard the story of how Saint's mother showed him this carving before she died, Clay understood how precious the painting would be to Saint. She'd loved this building, and it had been one of the driving factors in Saint's decision to buy and restore the place.

"That's kind of you. I know it'll mean a great deal to him."

Carlos blushed as he usually did when complimented, and they moved on to the fifth scene hand in hand. The Santa Monica Pier bustled with activity, and beyond the pier, different colored umbrellas dotted the sand while children ran and played in the sun. In the distance, over the Pacific, dark clouds were forming, and no one seemed to notice.

The contrast between the soft light of the foreground and dark menacing sky boiling behind the happy smiling faces caused a tangible feeling of dread. Carlos had the power to pull in the viewer, and it made Clay feel like he was a part of the painting. His man had an amazing gift.

"Is this how you felt after you saw Earl for the first time on the pier?" Clay asked.

Carlos's eyes widened as if he were surprised Clay got the reference so quickly. "Yeah. We'd had a wonderful day. Toes in the sand, laughing, eating, and playing the midway games, but all the while, Earl was waiting for us."

"In the background," Clay added. "Like a circling shark."

"We had no idea evil was that close," Carlos said.

"The smiling happy people." Clay pointed at the beachgoers. "You and me?" Carlos nodded, and Clay wrapped him in his arms. "You never have to worry about that again, sweetheart."

"It'll take time to push through those feelings."

The sixth painting was of the small airstream trailer where they'd played the Route 66 racing game. Bright, colorful lights popped, faceless people milled around, prizes hung from ropes seemingly in mid-air, and among all the chaos stood a little girl hugging a big white stuffy that barely fit into her arms. You couldn't see her expression, but the way the area had been highlighted against the evening sky and the swirl of the surrounding people made Clay feel hopeful.

"It gives me hope," Clay said. "I mean, looking at it, there's hope."

"You're right. It was my moment of hope."

Clay thought about it from Carlos's point of view. "The way the mom and little girl accepted your gift."

"Without fear."

He didn't need to say anything. Clay knew the pain it caused Carlos when people stared or backed away from him. His heart ached for the big man with a gentle soul.

The seventh and last painting sat on the table covered, making Clay wonder why Carlos had set it out if he wasn't sure.

"Those six are truly moving, poignant at times, and light and hopeful in others. The emotions they elicit are profound, and even though I'm about as far away from an art critic as a person can get, I believe many collectors will love these. You have an amazing talent."

Clay took Carlos into his arms and kissed him long and deep, reveling in the taste of his love. The word reverberated through his head: *love*. Couldn't be. It was way too soon for that. When he ended the kiss, Carlos's attention turned to the covered canvas, and Clay tucked that thought away to be examined later.

"I want to share this last one with you, though it isn't new. It hasn't been seen by anyone in a long time. Well, except for me."

Carlos pulled the cloth away, exposing a painting Clay thought had been destroyed after the *plein air* challenge since, according to the art articles he read about the piece, it had never been shown at any of the galleries or exhibitions where people purchased or viewed Carlos's work. The piece was of the rusted swing set in the derelict park Carlos had been taken to prove he could create original art and wasn't a forger out for a buck, but a victim of unscrupulous people.

Overgrown grass snaked and wound around rusted poles that were buried into the ground holding up the swing set. Old bottles and crumpled candy wrappers poked out from between blades of overgrown grass, striking an odd bit of color against the faded rusty scene. The set was designed to have two swings, but only the one remained, and even then, it barely clung to its corroded chains as it dangled in the wind.

The grooves in the ground underneath remained. Evidence of the numerous children who had swung from this piece of playground equipment before it was abandoned and left to decay. How long had it sat there alone, waiting for a child to come swing again he'll never know. The painting evoked strong emotions of sadness and loss, and Clay's heart ached looking at it. The surrounding buildings looked to be apartments, and he wondered how many kids were living in the neighborhood dreaming of having a working playground.

"This is the painting they forced you to create to prove you'd done the paintings in the show and that they were your originals," Clay said. "It's strange, but I feel the need to find that children's playground and save it. That site needs to be leveled and new equipment should be put in for the area's kids."

"It's not as strange as you think," Carlos said before placing his cellphone into Clay's hands and hitting play on a video.

The screen came to life, and Clay recognized the buildings in the background, but he looked up at the painting to confirm. This was the location where the old park had been. Instead of rust and disrepair, new colorful playground equipment stood, and children were waiting on the other side of the fence. Someone had fixed it up, which made him feel better.

It looked to be a dedication ceremony. There was cheering and a ribbon-cutting before the children were set loose to play to their heart's content. The video was shot by someone in the background who had an overview of the happenings.

"This is the same park?"

"Yeah, it is."

The video panned over to what looked to be a dedication monolith made of a stone four-foot by four-foot base that rose a couple of feet off the ground. A layer of wood rested on top of the stone, and a thick steel plaque topped it off. The person taking the video approached it and focused in on the engraving.

To me there is no picture so beautiful as smiling, bright-eyed, happy children;

no music so sweet as their clear and ringing laughter." P.T. Barnum

Dedicated to the children so that they may

create a beautiful picture or virtuoso of their own.

The Fernandez Foundation

"You," Clay said as he turned away from the screen. "You saved that park and playground after the critics made you *plein air* paint to prove your ability."

"I couldn't leave it the way it was. It didn't feel right. The same as you felt when you looked at my painting," Carlos explained. "I took the old playground equipment and incorporated it into the dedication pillar. The concrete base, wood from the old fence that used to surround it, and metal melted down into the top dedication plate."

"No one got left behind." Clay realized that this park meant more than simply a place to play. It was of rebirth and determination.

"Exactly."

"That's incredible. You're a philanthropist, yet you keep trying to convince me that you're no hero." Clay set down the phone and took Carlos into his arms once again, and once again the word *love* floated through his thoughts. He suspected it would be happening more often, and with greater frequency.

Chapter Twelve

The drive up the PCH was a never-ending palette of stunning scenery, from the Pacific Ocean to coppery, dust-colored hills that rose above the highway on its right side while beaches and beach houses stood to the left. Shops and restaurants spotted the ride, in some areas non-existent, and others packed together, from upscale restaurants such as Nobu, to the famous sought-after Malibu Seafood.

They stopped for a bite to eat at Casa Escobar in Malibu before continuing north. They ate two orders of Soft Taco Escobar Del Mar, which was made with mahi-mahi, fresh cabbage, tomato, onion, cilantro, and avocado. Still, the kicker was their Escobar chipotle aioli sauce. Carlos would buy it in bulk if he could.

The pitched ceiling was planked in dark wood, and the bright white walls held huge paintings of beach scenes. Chunky furniture and fresh seafood made Carlos feel like he was in Mexico. It was perfect. The excellent food and friendly service were topped only by the location: across the street from the Malibu Pier the restaurant was the ideal stop for tourists and locals alike. He wanted to sit out on the patio at night listening to music and drinking top-shelf tequila. They lived close enough to come up any time they wanted, and there were hotels close by so indulging meant a drunken stroll back to their room.

They'd intended to get an early start, but he'd sidetracked them for a couple of hours. After sharing his work with Clay, they'd sat on the couch talking for a while before finally going to the car to head out. They'd shared some of the more challenging moments of their childhoods, to the dreams they had for the future. They never lacked for conversation even though neither of them was known for being talkative or particularly communicative. Their connection provided the impetus to share, and their quiet moments were some of his favorites.

Like now, with Clay driving and Carlos busy taking pictures, they didn't say much, but when one of them spoke, the other paid attention. Their windows were down, and the sun was streaming into the car. The Pacific Ocean crashing onto the shore was their music as they drove toward Santa Barbara. At times, the mountains provided sharp relief, and the canyons wove up into the hills where houses were perched precariously. Carlos now understood how easily a landslide could decimate the area.

In places, the terrain became rocky with mountains and cliffs led down to the beaches below. They stopped at Point Dume in Northern Malibu to walk a bit of the park and go down to its white sand beach, where they stood hand in hand with their toes in the sand. A bit further up the PCH, the terrain seemed to level out once they passed the Point Mugu State Park. Shortly after, they had to turn off the PCH to get the 101 to head up to Santa Barbara. For a short time, the freeway was like any other, but after they cleared Ventura, the Pacific sat alongside the road, gracing them with unparalleled views.

Carlos had his head on a swivel the entire drive. He'd never been on road trips and didn't pretend to have a clue about areas beyond his limited reach. Each stop with their postcard views, piers, and diverse people fascinated him. He couldn't get enough. He'd been right all those years ago when he imagined getting in a car and driving Route 66. Road trips were his thing, and he couldn't wait for more.

Throughout their journey, Clay would pull off the PCH to show him interesting places, beaches that seemed private, but weren't— every beach in California was public— and he'd point at sights and tell Carlos what they were. The simple joy they were sharing was worth more to Carlos than anything money could buy.

As they neared Santa Barbara, or the American Riviera as it was called, Carlos fell in love with the architecture, which had a heavy Spanish Colonial feel. White stucco walls, barrel-tiled rooves, Saltillo tiled floors, dark polished woods and exposed beamed ceilings were constants in the area architecture. He couldn't wait to get a closer look around once they reached The Californian Hotel. Clay had suggested Carlos choose the hotel, and he'd reserved a suite at the stunning, nearly century-old hotel.

"Now's the time to tell me which hotel we are staying at so I can get off the right exit from the freeway."

"I reserved a suite at The Californian."

"The Californian? Now that'll be a first. I'm not sure the clothes I brought are fancy enough for that place." Clay grinned.

"Neither do I, but I don't care." Carlos chuckled.

"Have you ever been there?" Clay asked.

"No."

"Then what made you choose it?" Clay took the off-ramp to Garden Street.

"A long time ago, I swore to myself that if I ever got out of that room, if I ever made it, I would learn how to enjoy the rest of the life I was given. I sat in isolation for years after making a name for myself in the art world. When I moved to DTLA, it was my chance at keeping that promise to my younger self. It doesn't mean I want to see or stay in all the most expensive places, but years ago I saw The Californian in an advertisement, and it's been stuck in my head ever since. Now that we're together, I have the chance to share all those dreams with you."

"When you put it that way, let's get our butts over into the luxury lane. This should be fun," Clay smiled wide, making Carlos feel like he was on top of the world.

Carlos reached over and squeezed Clay's thigh. "Thank you. I knew you'd understand."

***

When Clay pulled up outside the lobby of a hotel so big it took up a couple of blocks, he admitted to being nervous. The vibrant barrel-tiled rooves struck a sharp contrast to the bright white stucco walls, which made the hotel fit in with the overall Santa Barbara theme. He parked his car and waited as a valet and porter headed in their direction.

At first, Clay thought they were coming out to tell him to move, but to his surprise, the porter grabbed a luggage cart, and the valet came over to the driver's door with his valet ticket in hand. Neither gave his 2016 Mazda a second look. They treated him as if he drove in with a Bentley.

When Carlos had told him where they were staying, Clay felt trepidation. He'd been raised so far from comfort he didn't understand what the word meant until the Everetts took him in. He never imagined he'd find himself in one of the suites at a high-end hotel. He thought he was more likely to be called to the scene of a crime in a hotel this swanky than ever be a guest in one.

After Carlos explained why he chose this place, Clay swore to himself he'd never deny his man what he needed. All those years living like a recluse, never enjoying the money he earned, Carlos deserved anything and everything his heart desired. After the hell his life had been, if Carlos wanted to buy a ticket to the moon, Clay would stand by his side, albeit clutching a motion sickness bag.

Clay pushed the button to open the hatch for the porter before stepping out. He looked over at Carlos to find his man already in conversation with the guy. No sign of the shy, reserved person he saw having a panic attack on the sidewalk near The Gates. Clay handed a tip along with his car keys to the waiting valet.

"Thank you, sir. If you need your vehicle at any time, call down to valet, and we'll bring it up front for you."

"Thank you." Clay looked down at his nametag. "Ricardo."

The porter shut the hatchback, and Ricardo pulled away as Clay made his way over to Carlos's side.

"This place is amazing," Carlos gushed while pointing things out with exaggerated arm movements, making both Clay and the porter smile.

"Sirs, if you'd please follow me, I'll take you to check-in."

"Thank you, Daniel," Carlos said as he reached for Clay's hand, which he immediately gave. "Isn't it beautiful?"

"I have to admit, it's pretty spectacular." At first, Clay didn't think he'd be able to get comfortable here, but now, he couldn't wait to explore the grounds. "It's a welcomed surprise."

"Daniel told me about a place not far from here named Hook and Press. He said we have to try their donuts."

"Well, that we can do." Clay chuckled as the two of them followed Daniel into the lobby.

The black and white tile matched the black and white pillars in the lobby area. High-back chairs and heavy wooden furniture gave way to brightly colored chairs and large arched windows. The various designs used to create the moldings on the ceiling brought the whole area together. The interior motif was different from the barrel-tiled roof and white stucco walls outside, and Clay had never seen anything like it before.

Check-in was a breeze, and soon they were following Daniel up to the Magellan Suite. After everything they'd seen so far, Clay had no idea what to expect. Carlos looked ready to burst with excitement, making Clay's heart beat faster at the joy pouring off his man.

Daniel stopped outside a door that Clay assumed was theirs, unlocked it, and held it open for them to enter. Over twelve-hundred square feet was a lot of space. Black and white tile ran across the living and dining room walls at about waist height. Clay hadn't ever seen that before. It fit in with everything else, even the living room fireplace. This place was top-notch and so far above his pay grade it wasn't funny.

Carlos sat in one of the armchairs to test it out while Clay tried the couch. Beautiful paintings and a large flatscreen hung on the wall. The dining table sat six people. Their patio faced the Santa Ynez Mountains making a stunning and perfect view.

In the bedroom there was a king-sized bed, dressers, and more chairs. The bathroom was all marble. Everywhere he looked, thick grey veins weaved through the marble on the floor, walls, shower, and vanity. The walk-in shower was big enough to accommodate the two of them comfortably.

Daniel had set their bags at the foot of the bed and said, "Do you have any questions, sirs?"

Carlos asked, "I was hoping to get a reservation for two to the Blackbird for dinner tomorrow night. Would the concierge be the best way to inquire if it's still possible?"

"I will be happy to have concierge look into that for you."

"Great, thank you," Carlos pulled out his wallet, and handed Daniel a generous tip. "You've been really helpful."

Daniel didn't look down. He nodded and said, "If I can be of any more service, please call the front desk."

Moments later they were alone, standing in a suite in Santa Barbara, a short walk to the beach. "So, what would you like to do first, sweetheart?"

"I'd like to explore the hotel and maybe walk to Stearns Wharf," Carlos suggested.

"Anything you want."

***

They'd found the rooftop pool, the spa, the bar, several patios scattered throughout for relaxing, the Goat Tree Café, and something called the Funk Zone encompassing a large area in the surrounding streets. They'd sworn to come back and check it out another time because the Wharf was beckoning.

Carlos was still riding the high from all the excitement and couldn't wipe the smile from his face as they walked down State Street to the harbor. The day had started on a high note and never came down. If this was what it meant to have a lust for life, Carlos couldn't wait to explore whatever came next.

This was what Carlos had dreamt of when he'd been locked away. This right here. The freedom to explore places, make friends, sit on a patio for dinner or drinks without fear or having to look over his shoulder all the time. Without expecting and receiving the worst life had to offer.

He didn't take for granted Clay's part in all of this happiness. As they neared the Dolphin Fountain and beach leading onto the pier, Carlos couldn't think of a better time to ask a question he'd been sitting on for days.

"No pressure or anything, but I want you to move in with me. I know it's early on in our relationship, and we have a lot more to learn about each other, but the thought of you leaving now guts me." There, he said it. Now what?

Clay grabbed him by his shoulders and leaned him against the railing of the pier. "You want me to stay?"

"More than anything."

"I didn't want to leave you either. I love you."

Carlos felt his legs go weak but managed to stay upright. "I love you, too. I never said anything because I worried you'd think I was crazy."

"Then we're both crazy." Clay's smile said it all. "Crazy in love."

Carlos lunged forward and took Clay into his arms before spinning him around in circles. He'd never felt this happy, and he wasn't quite sure what to do with all this energy.

"Save some of that for later," Clay teased. "I have plans for you."

Oh yeah. He liked Clay's plans.

After another round of kisses, they managed to pull themselves together and continued down the pier. Off to the right was a marina with speedboats, tall-mast sailboats, and yachts.

Roughly one-third of the way down the pier, they came to Stearns Wharf and the first restaurant, The Harbor, where seafood, of course, was their specialty.

Cars could drive onto the pier, and there were several places to park. Further on, the walking area became quite a bit larger with the Santa Barbara Museum of Natural History Sea Center and more restaurants and shopping. Since the Sea Center was closed, they went right and wandered through the gift shop, passed the ice cream and candy shops, and headed to a big brown building with a whale painted on the side. Moby Dick Restaurant.

Clay's stomach growled, and Carlos's joined along. "What do you think?" Carlos asked as he tilted his head at the building. "Wanna have dinner here tonight?"

Clay took a look at the place before saying, "I'm game. Lead on."

The interior of the building was decorated in light woods and a dark carpet. There were various tchotchkes and fishing paraphernalia here and there, but the item that got his attention was the front half of a giant shark hanging on the wall. It had to be six feet long, and that only went to its gills. Its jaws gaped open, showcasing rows of sharp teeth.

"Mascot?" Carlos asked.

"You got me. Is it real?"

Carlos shrugged. "I'm not sure. Let's sit on the patio."

They were soon seated out on the patio in the warm California sun listening to the seagulls while watching boats sail in the distance. At times Carlos found it hard to accept that these places were real.

"Can't get much better than this," Clay remarked as he took hold of Carlos's hand. "Beautiful day out with the handsome man I love."

"I've never been so happy," Carlos said.

"Good. I want you to stay that way." Clay squeezed his hand.

"With you around, how can I not be?"

Their waiter came and went, and their crab arrived a short time later as the two men watched the sunset from their table. Carlos basked not only in the sun's waning rays but in the knowledge that Clay loved him.

He was a thirty-three-year-old man, and that was the first time Carlos ever had anyone aside from his brother say those words to him.

This love was precious.

Carlos and Clay loved each other.

That was all that mattered.

Chapter Thirteen

Clay wasn't sure it was the beans or the location, but he'd never had a coffee this rich before. They were finishing up with breakfast out on their private patio while looking out at the mountain range.

"Did you call valet to bring the car around?" Carlos asked without turning to look at him. Instead, he was transfixed by their surroundings. Clay didn't mind. Santa Barbara was living up to its moniker of being the American Riviera.

"Yeah. I told them we'd be down in twenty minutes."

"I can't wait to take a tour of the Old Mission," Carlos said. "I read it's considered the Queen of Missions because it's so beautiful."

His love looked ready to take flight while he was going through the visitors' guide for the area. Clay kept reminding himself Carlos never had accessed the world before. The thought of seeing a two-hundred-year-old mission was like hitting the tourist jackpot.

Through everything they'd seen and done, Carlos wore a look of wonder about him, and it was beginning to rub off onto Clay. Things he'd seen a thousand times over now shone like freshly polished silver. Carlos was breathing new life into Clay, making him question who the real tour guide was.

Through his love's eyes, the world around him sprung to life, bringing him out of his own hibernation of sorts. He hadn't realized that after his ex-fiancé had sucker-punched him in the heart that his life had turned monochrome. Nothing had been left to add to color until now.

"Yep, I know. But I think I'll have a better appreciation of it with you by my side," Clay admitted. "You about done with your coffee?"

With one quick gulp, Carlos emptied his cup and turned to face Clay. "Thank you." His expression was full of emotion, and Clay couldn't help but reach over and take him into a long hug.

"In such a short time, you've become the most important person in my life. I love you and want to spend all my time by your side."

"Forever?"

"Forever." It didn't scare Clay to say that. Nothing had felt as real as what they had. Their kiss was sweet and over way too soon, as they all were. "Okay, let's hit the streets and go visit a mission."

The drive over took less than twenty minutes, and he was happily surprised to find ample free public parking. He noticed Mission Park located alongside the mission, full of trees and flowers, and a memorial rose garden. They'd have to take a walk through before they left.

"Excited?" Clay asked, already knowing the answer.

"Yeah." Carlos smiled. "This getaway has been perfect. Thank you."

"I'd take you to see the entire globe if that were possible, sweetheart."

After another quick kiss, they got out of their car and headed over to the mission. Tour signs were leading them, but when they reached the front, they had to stop to take in the twin bell towers. The six pillar-like structures built into the stonework appeared almost pink in the sunlight, along with the trim and bell towers' rooves.

"It's even better than the pictures," Carlos said as he snapped a few photos.

"It is awe-inspiring. I believe it had to be rebuilt a couple of times over the years due to earthquakes," Clay mentioned as they stood among a growing crowd of tourists.

"I can't wait to see inside." Carlos grabbed Clay's hand and took off toward the entrance. Clay couldn't help but laugh at the joy this man was experiencing and was sharing with him.

The tour took them through the history of the mission. From the church to the Sacred Garden, arched hallways and doors, mausoleums, graveyard, artifacts, and the Franciscan monks' robes, Clay watched Carlos soak it all up like a sponge. Clay couldn't help but think of all the people that drove by this place every day, taking living here for granted.

"I'd love to stop by the gift shop," Carlos said as he snapped a picture of the water fountain in the center of the Sacred Garden. "Maybe we can get a memento of our visit."

"Sounds good," Clay agreed.

Carlos went still.

"What's wrong?" Clay glanced around the garden and walking paths. There were two families to the left walking in the opposite direction, an older man sitting on a bench in the shade twenty yards away, and what looked to be a group of students on a class trip. Nothing stood out.

Carlos shook his head and pulled out his map. "It's nothing. For a moment, that older man sitting over there reminded me of Earl and I froze. I know logically that's impossible, right?"

Clay understood that fear and knew it would take time for Carlos to become comfortable with the idea that Earl Roy was dead. They walked into the gift shop, which was crowded with the school group.

"You don't have to worry. I read the coroner's report. Earl isn't coming back from a gunshot through his right temple." Clay made sure to keep his voice low, not wanting to freak out anyone.

They moved over to the educational section, and Carlos was eyeing the *Inside the California Missions* DVD when he turned to look Clay in the eyes.

"Right temple?"

"It appears that way. The gun was in his right hand."

"Earl Roy was left-handed."

Alarm bells started sounding in Clay's head. "Left-handed. You're sure."

"After so many whoopings, trust me, I know his dominant hand."

Clay pulled out his cellphone. "I have to call the captain. They need to know about this." The noise level in the gift shop seemed to rise. "We have to step outside so I can make the call."

Carlos looked down at the DVD in his hand. It was the last one on the shelf. "I'll go pay for this and come find you."

"I don't like leaving you alone."

"Back through the door is the Sacred Garden. I'll go directly there once I'm cashed out," he said while looking around. "There is no one in here who could pose a threat to me."

Clay looked around as well, and other than the staff and kids hurrying to use their spending money while the exhausted teachers tried to get a handle on them, they were alone. "Okay. It looks safe. But the moment you've paid, I'll be right on the other side of that door." He pointed at the old wooden door leading back inside the mission.

"Perfect. Go make your call. It might be important to the case," Carlos said before stepping a few feet away and getting into the checkout line. "Go."

With one final look around, Clay returned to the door and stepped back through. His fingers couldn't dial fast enough. The information that Earl was left-handed and would have likely used his dominant hand to hold the gun had to be shared.

There still might be a killer out there.

***

Carlos realized his mistake the moment something cold and hard was pressed into his lower back.

"Put the DVD down and walk out of the exterior doors to the parking lot, or I start shooting," a man said.

"You wouldn't get away with it in here," Carlos challenged. He wasn't going to be a victim anymore.

"Who knows? In the ensuing chaos, one of LAPD's finest might have to make the ultimate sacrifice to save the children." The threat was real, and that kids might get hurt made Carlos decide to cooperate.

He set the DVD down on a nearby shelf and walked out the doors opposite from where Clay had gone. Though he hadn't turned around to look at his kidnapper, Carlos knew the voice well enough.

"Why are you doing this, Jeremy?"

"Me? You're the one that started all this," Jeremy growled as he led them to a heavily tinted Suburban. "Get in. You're driving."

Carlos opened the unlocked door and slid in behind the wheel while his manager sat in the backseat with the barrel of the gun pointed at Carlos's head. Jeremy threw him the keys, and he pulled out of the parking lot. In the rearview mirror, Carlos saw Clay running out of the gift shop before turning the corner. Then he lost sight of his lover, and they were heading to who knew where.

After a few turns down streets he didn't recognize and miles away from Clay, Jeremy said, "Pull over up in that parking lot by the Walgreens and get into the passenger seat."

He drove where he was told, shifted the vehicle in park, and with effort, he moved his body over the console to the passenger side of the vehicle. Before he had a chance to make a break for it out the passenger door, Carlos felt a sharp prick to his neck and turned to see Jeremy holding a syringe.

"Night, night, painter boy."

Those last two words rang in his mind before his world went dark. That was what Earl used to call him.

Shit. He was a dead man.

***

Carlos woke sometime later with a pounding headache. Whatever Jeremy had used on him sure packed a punch, and he wondered how long he'd been out. He knew by now Clay was searching for him, and the police had been notified, meaning Miguel would know.

He looked around at the room he was in and was happy to find he was alone. Even though he suspected the only door was locked, he tried turning the handle anyway without success. He reached into his pocket to find his cellphone was missing, so he scanned the room for any means of escape.

The area he was in wasn't overly dirty, but dust had settled over the floor, and the state of the fixtures told him nobody had been here in a while. The likelihood of him being found was slimmer if he was in an abandoned building.

He let out a deep breath and realized he wasn't afraid. He wasn't on the verge of a panic attack, and his mind wasn't racing in a million different directions. He was calmly analyzing his options and making plans for when Jeremy returned. A first he could credit to being loved and knowing he was worth loving.

He was furious for being taken away at gunpoint and locked up, and he desperately wanted to get back to Clay, but his ability to think this out wasn't as impaired as it would've been six months ago. Why would Jeremy wish to hurt him, and how did he know about the nickname Earl had given him?

All questions he'd ask once the bastard showed up, which, as it turned out, wasn't long. He heard keys jingling outside the locked door. Carlos stepped back and waited for his chance to take a run at the door once it was open, but the barrel of a gun poking through first had him rethinking that idea.

Jeremy walked into the room with a middle-aged blonde woman by his side, waving his handgun around like he was searching for something to shoot. Asshole.

"Ah, you're awake, good," he laughed. "I'd hate to have to carry you again."

"Gee, sorry to put you out." His time of taking people's shit was long over.

"So, you're Carlos Fernandez," the woman said. "Somehow, I expected you to be cowering in the corner, as Earl had predicted."

"You know Earl Roy? Who the hell are you?" Carlos didn't recognize her.

"I'm the grieving widow, Sally Roy." She moved her hands in a flourish any Vegas showgirl would be proud of. At least the ones he's seen on those travel shows.

"Grieving widow, my ass. Which one of you pulled the trigger on the old scumbag?" The more he knew, the more he hoped to find some way out of this.

"I have to admit, that was me," Sally said in almost a singsong voice. "But I can't take all the credit. Jeremy helped."

"Why are you doing this?"

"You remember the day I approached you about becoming your manager?" Jeremy asked.

"Yeah." How could he forget it? "A couple months before I'd finished painting for the critics." That was one of the low points in his life, and when Jeremy had approached him about a long-term contract saying all the right things, he bought into it. As his manager, Jeremy promised to take care of everything so Carlos could stay away from the limelight, and until now, Carlos had never questioned Jeremy's intentions or honesty.

"Well, that wasn't the first time we'd met, but you were much younger than the previous times. I can understand you not recognizing me since I used to have dark hair and a long beard when you were a child."

Carlos looked closer at Jeremy minus his balding gray hair and clean-shaven face, and it took only a few moments for the image to snap into place. "Jeremy Redding."

"Well, Jeremy Randolf, now, as you already know." His laugh was cruel as Carlos realized who he'd been working with for over a decade.

"You were one of Earl's associates back in the day." Carlos had seen him on those rare occasions where his foster parents dragged out their golden goose to show off to the people making money from his suffering.

Carlos lunged forward, but Jeremy was quick to raise his gun. "Now, now, big guy. You in a hurry to die?"

"You fucking piece of shit. If I ever get my hands on you—"

"Yeah, yeah. Pitiful threats in your position. I used to set up buyers from all over the world. Imagine my luck when I came upon you years later trying to make all the big bad people believe you were a real artist." His voice dripped with sarcasm.

"Why risk me recognizing you and turning you in?"

"Money," Jeremy laughed. "Of course. I saw what you could do and how fragile you were. It was so easy to make you believe I wanted to help you when everyone else didn't trust you."

"How did Earl end up involved in this?" Was this set up before the bastard went to prison?

"You might not have recognized me, but that old bastard had," Jeremy growled. "Earl saw my face in an interview I'd done on your behalf, so we were forced to cut him in."

"We?" He assumed that meant Jeremy and Sally, but who knew how many were involved. There'd been a lot of associates over the years.

"Me and my soon-to-be wife." Jeremy wrapped his arm around Sally's waist before squeezing her ass. Sally had to be in her forties while Jeremy and Earl were both in their sixties.

"I thought you were married to Earl?"

"It was the only way to keep tabs on the lunatic," Sally groaned. "I'd bring him information from Jeremy, top-up his bank account, and give him an updated balance of his share."

"You shared your percentage of the sales of my work?"

"Not exactly."

"How much have you been skimming off my earnings?"

"A good thirty percent."

"You fucking bastard."

"Hey, what did you care? You never used the money. It sat there accruing interest until now. I took it out and used it as normal people do."

"Normal people don't steal and kill," Carlos said. "And what the hell do you mean by now?"

"Your bullshit return to public life and relationship with an LAPD officer forced my hand. You couldn't leave things the way they were. Soon enough, you'd want more control over your financial affairs, you would've noticed the mystery withdrawals, and then it would all be over. All the years and my hard work wasted."

"Your hard work? You've got to be kidding me. You've lived like a leech attached to me since my childhood. What the fuck do you know about real work?" Carlos was ready to blow.

"I've had to maintain appearances, attend charity events and gallery showings on your behalf. It was exhausting."

This time Sally took a good long look at Jeremy. "You partied and played up to all those rich and famous people," she said, sneering. "You never once had to deal with the dirty bits like Earl Roy."

"Speaking of my dead foster father, did you kill him for the money?"

"No." Sally laughed. "The idiot could've taken the money and disappeared, but no. The asshole had to follow you and risk our entire operation. He was obsessed with you and likely would've taken a shot if I hadn't stepped in."

"Forgive me for not thanking you." Carlos knew Sally had to be as insane as the rest of them. "So, what's the plan now?"

"The plan is for you to disappear," Jeremy said.

"Then how will the two of you continue to make money if I'm no longer around to paint?" Carlos wouldn't ever be painting anything for Jeremy again, not because Carlos would disappear, but because Jeremy and Sally would be behind bars. Carlos was *not* giving up what it took so long to get.

"Don't worry about us, Carlos," his former manager said. "We'll be fine with the life insurance money, and of course, being sole beneficiaries of your will should provide us with a lush life."

"What? I don't have life insurance or a will."

By the cocky smile on Jeremy's face, Carlos knew he was wrong. "You really should review each page of the paperwork you sign, painter boy." Sally laughed.

"Let me get this straight. Sally is now the beneficiary of Earl's portion, and you're the beneficiary of my estate if anything ever happens to me. Don't you think all that is going to seem a bit strange? Maybe bring up a few questions, especially if you marry Earl's widow."

"It's all legal," Jeremy stated. "Besides, we won't be in the country long."

"Except the part where you committed fraud, embezzled money, killed Earl, and if I'm staying with the plot here, my death as well."

"All necessities. Now it's time for us to go," Jeremy said as he motioned with the gun for Carlos to move to the door.

Carlos walked to the door and was halfway through when he heard the gunshot. It took him a moment to realize he hadn't been shot, and he turned around to find Jeremy's body crumpled on the floor in the center of an ever-expanding pool of red.

He didn't know what to do, so he froze to the spot waiting for Sally to shoot him as well. It crushed him to think he'd never see his brother and Clay again.

"Keep moving, unless you want to lay down beside him," she ordered while pointing the gun at him. Where had she been hiding that?

"Didn't want to split the money two ways? Don't get me wrong, I'm not torn up about Jeremy being dead, merely curious."

"The blow-hard deserved it. God, he never shut up. While Jeremy was out partying with the rich folks on worldwide tours, I had to deal with that perverted old man. They can both rot in hell for all I care. Now move, we have a plane to catch."

Carlos continued down the hallway, trying to think of a way out of this because there was no way he was getting onto any damn plane, especially with this murderous crazy woman.

"Where are we going?" Keep her talking. Look for your moment.

"You'd be surprised how many no-name out in the middle of nowhere airfields there are. There's a dozen off the top of my head where we can fly under the radar, land, and bury your body."

"We? Didn't you just kill the we?" Who the hell else was involved in this?

"Oh, honey, how naïve are you? Jeremy wasn't ever part of my future."

They stepped outside into the cool evening air, allowing Carlos his first opportunity to take in their location. Everywhere he looked, there was desert sand. He'd been kept in a large hangar, and the only light for miles was coming from the small plane waiting for them.

Someone came around the back of the small aircraft, and Carlos got his first look at Sally's accomplice. He was young, maybe twenty-five, and looked to be the quintessential surfer dude, complete with long blond hair, shark tooth necklace, and board shorts. Could this get any more stereotypical?

Chapter Fourteen

Clay sat stone-faced in the passenger seat of a squad car as their team raced toward Carlos. The kidnapper had gotten a couple of hours' head start, but they were making up that time fast. They were headed to a location east of Barstow, California, where the tracker he'd hidden on Carlos led them.

He knew Carlos would be furious after he'd made it clear to Miguel that he wouldn't wear a tracker and Clay went behind his back and planted one on him. Of course, he'd contacted Miguel and the Captain when he realized Carlos was missing from the gift shop. They were among the other vehicles following behind them.

As they neared the area, they abandoned their vehicles and went in on foot to give them a better chance of approaching the buildings unseen and catching the kidnappers unaware. It was their best hope of getting Carlos back alive.

How could he expect Carlos to forgive him after this, when Clay knew he'd never forgive himself?

***

Carlos looked at the surfer in disbelief. "He's the pilot?"

"Hey, babe, ready to go?" The new arrival said to Sally as they neared.

"Sure he is," she answered. "His flying ability isn't what you should be worried about."

"Man, you sure you want to do this 'cause at the rate Sally's dropping partners, you're not going to get a chance to see a dime of whatever she's promised," Carlos said as they stopped beside a four-seater plane with faded yellow lines down the sides.

"What?" he asked while looking between Carlos and Sally.

"Don't pay any attention to him," Sally crooned while using her free hand to rub the surfer boy's chest. "He'd say anything to get out of this."

"Listen, surfer dude, obviously you're good with me being shot, but I wonder if Earl and Jeremy would agree it was worth it. Oh wait, can't ask them 'cause they're dead. Go inside and take a look if you don't believe me. Pool of blood, stiff guy in the middle of it dead as a doornail. Got yourself mixed up with a real black widow here."

Sally jammed the gun into his side. "Shut up and get in the plane."

"No. I'm not getting on that plane. You'll have to kill me here." It kind of surprised him that they hadn't already, but they were unhinged, so making sense of their thought process was beyond his comprehension.

"Wait, what about the old dude? Where's he?" the surfer asked, looking a bit more concerned now that it sounded like a one-way trip for him as well. The guy pushed forward, forcing Sally to look at him. "Tell me."

Carlos took his chance by shoving Sally's accomplice into her, making both of them fall to the ground, then he took off toward the hangar because there wasn't anywhere else around to hide. It was a large building, and he needed a weapon if he had a prayer of getting out of there alive.

He heard a gunshot but didn't stop until he was deep inside the building. When he turned a corner, he found himself in a large area packed with planes and pieces of aircraft. It was like a labyrinth as he made his way through piles of metal, parts, and a few wings. Another shot rang out, this time a lot closer.

"Give up," Sally screamed. "You're not leaving here alive."

Carlos hid behind what looked like engine blocks, but he was no mechanic. He might've seen one on the television once. The metal looked thick and could probably stop a bullet. He hoped.

Suddenly the area outside lit up with flashlights. "Come out with your hands up. This is the Barstow Police Department. We have the building surrounded."

Clay had found him. Carlos would have cheered if it didn't give away his position. He was prepared to hide until the police found him. The last thing he wanted to do was accidentally run into the crazy woman while trying to get outside to the waiting rescue party.

The officer with the loudspeaker repeated his warning, and other than an occasional scrape of metal, Carlos heard nothing. Where could she have gone? Had she found a way out? He took a chance and stood, wanting a quick look in case the coast was clear. It had been the wrong decision.

"Thought you could get away, didn't you?" Her cold, biting voice sent chills up Carlos's back.

"There are police officers all over the place. It's over, Sally." She had to see that.

"What do I care? What's one more murder charge on top of three?"

So that confirmed surfer had been the shot when Carlos was running back into the building. Sally's eyes bulged from their sockets as a twisted smile made her face more horrific. There didn't seem to be any sanity left inside of her to try and reason with.

She raised her gun and pointed it straight at Carlos's chest. "Say hi to Earl for me."

Carlos closed his eyes as she moved to pull the trigger. He didn't want to see the bullet coming that would end his life. His body was shoved to the side and down onto the floor. When Carlos opened his eyes, he found himself staring straight into Clay's beautiful azure blue pools. When Carlos looked to the side, Sally was on the ground, having her hands cuffed behind her back by several officers.

Something wet brushed against his right hand behind Clay's back, and he lifted it to find it covered in blood. The fact that he wasn't in pain hit home at the same moment that he realized the blood was coming from Clay.

"You're shot." Oh, fuck. He took the bullet meant for Carlos. "We need help over here. Officer down," Carlos hollered, trying to get anyone's attention. "Is it bad?"

"Nothing to worry about, sweetheart." Clay's voice was strained, making Carlos worry all the more. "I love you, Carlos."

A large red box was slammed down beside them as the paramedics took over. In the background, Carlos could hear Miguel's voice, but refused to break eye contact with Clay. "I love you too."

Then Clay terrified Carlos.

He closed his eyes.

Epilogue

Carlos looked up from his canvas at the scene before him, happy with the way his painting was progressing. The wind blew through his hair and played with the American flag hanging outside Seligman Sundries in Seligman, Arizona. The mix of old and new Route 66 signs attached to the outside of the green building only brought more depth to his painting of the historic sight.

An old red gas pump stood to the right, and yellow hand-painted signs boasting they had coffee, jewelry, gifts, and a museum, all hung over the front entrance. Directional signs set on poles on either side of the building proclaimed the distances to places like Rome, Bangkok, Paris, and London. The front half of an old car stuck out of the front of the building, and an old, rusted tow-truck sat waiting for the next call for help. Someone had even attached a pair of buckteeth to the front radiator, reminding Carlos of a cartoon he'd seen.

In all of his dreaming about Historic Route 66, he never imagined how meaningful it would be to make the drive. Carlos thought about all the people throughout the nineteen twenties, thirties, and forties who'd travelled this route on their way to California before more significant highways were built.

Honestly, after everything that'd happened to him, and the lives that were lost, the fact that he was still around was a miracle.

"You want some coffee?" Clay asked from the doorway of their new luxury motorhome. When they wanted to tour around in a less cumbersome vehicle they parked the motorhome in a secured facility and rented a car.

"Sure, I'm about done here for today."

While he packed away his easel and cleaned his paintbrushes, Clay joined him with two steaming coffee mugs. He sat down in the folding camp chair beside Carlos and groaned as he stretched out his legs.

"How are you feeling? Any pain?" Carlos asked, ever in tune with his man's movements and noises.

Clay had been shot in the back, saving Carlos's life. He'd physically thrown himself in front of the bullet for him. When Clay had closed his eyes and lost consciousness Carlos had thought the worst. He'd begun to panic and had to be restrained by his brother, as well as Ross, Sam, and Captain Meyers while Clay was being worked on. Even though logically he'd known the paramedics needed room to do their job, he couldn't bear to be separated from Clay.

Thanks to those paramedics, who hadn't given up, they were able to stabilize him for the helicopter ride to the nearest trauma hospital. The bullet had pierced Clay's liver, after cracking three vertebrae in his spine. Thankfully it didn't nick the cord, and had missed his right lung by millimeters. Clay had already been through two surgeries with more to come, but he never complained, which concerned Carlos. It was human nature to complain from pain, but Clay had never bitched and moaned about it.

"I'm good," he said. "A little stiff. How's your latest work going? You seem to be getting into this *plein air* painting." Carlos didn't miss the subject change.

Carlos had decided that once it was safe to take Clay away from his doctors for an extended period, he'd show his love all the places he remembered seeing in those old Route 66 magazines as a child. Clay was off work until he was medically sound to return, so the trip was part of his rest and relaxation as he recovered. The motorhome allowed Clay to lay down when his back was sore no matter where they were, and being away from hospitals and doctors helped him relax.

A new series of paintings titled Return to The Mother Road, which paid homage to John Steinbeck's *The Grapes of Wrath,* was in the works as they explored as many original places on the historic route as they could.

Some of the route no longer existed, gone with the new highways. Carlos wanted to capture as much of it as he could before it disappeared. Places like this sundry store, the Cadillac Ranch, Wigwam Motel, Calico Ghost Town, gas stations, and so much more. There was even the world's largest catsup bottle in Illinois to immortalize.

"I'll make sure the heating pad is set up in bed tonight. I'll help loosen the muscles in your back."

"You're an angel, sweetheart," Clay said before taking a drink of his coffee. "I might try one of those over-the-counter muscle relaxants before bed as well." He'd been prescribed much heavier pain medication, but refused to take it unless he was laid out in bed and couldn't get up.

"Whatever you need to do, I'm right here to help," Carlos told him. "Do you need me to go to the store and pick some up?"

"Nah. I still have a bottle in the bathroom," he said with a smile. "Hear from your brother today?" Off topic again. Clay didn't like talking about his pain.

"I swear he calls every day," Carlos huffed, allowing Clay to duck out of a conversation he didn't want to have.

"He loves you and worries about you." Clay chuckled.

"He's not calling to check up on me," he explained. "It's you he's worried about."

Clay chuckle turned into a cough causing him almost to spill his coffee down the front of his jeans. "Me?"

"Yeah, you. *'How's Clay feeling? Are you helping him enough? Make sure he rests. If Clay needs a doctor, we'll send a helicopter for him. He'll need his doctors here, not someone out in the middle of nowhere. Is he eating enough?'* On and on. Seriously, I can't make this shit up. Suddenly I'm completely capable of taking care of myself, and it's you he's handling with kid gloves. He's calling me because he doesn't want to bother you in case you're resting."

Miguel had done a complete one-eighty when it came to Clay. No longer was he concerned if the man was good enough for Carlos. Now Miguel behaved as if Clay could do no wrong.

Clay had risked his life to save Carlos, and that must've convinced Miguel of Clay's worth. Carlos had known what kind of man Clay was from the beginning, and could've done without the bullet to prove it.

"Well, isn't that… um… sweet?" Clay looked lost for words.

"Miguel has adopted you, my love, and there's nothing you can do about it. Now he can put all of his worrying and overreacting on you. I'm happy to bow out."

"Damn. I didn't get any say in this," Clay grumbled.

Carlos couldn't help but chuckle as he leaned back in his chair and took a drink of his coffee. The delicious brew was their new favorite blend, thanks to the Californian Hotel. Clay had loved it the first time they'd visited the hotel, and Carlos made sure he had a constant supply ever since.

"Clay," he said. "Why are you avoiding discussing your pain with me?" Carlos was worried Clay could be in severe pain, and he'd never know due to Clay's misguided effort to spare Carlos the worry, which worried him more.

"Not a whole lot to talk about," Clay said. "I'm in pain. Sometimes it's worse than others. Nothing I can't handle."

"But I want to help you handle it," Carlos insisted. "Do it together."

Clay turned in his chair to look at Carlos. "You're helping me through all of this. Don't ever doubt that. With you, I have the love and security I need to heal. You give me the strength to push harder and to never stop. You're the one I look to for support, and you give it to me in spades. I don't focus on the pain. It's manageable. In time, I'll heal, and it'll be a dim memory. You are worth every moment of discomfort I have. I love you."

Carlos's heart overflowed with love for the strong, resilient, and amazing man in front of him. He wasn't sure what his life would have looked like if he hadn't met Clay the day of the wedding, and he didn't want to know. From victim, prisoner, and self-imposed exile, to survivor, lover, and beloved, Carlos was living his best life with the man of his dreams by his side.

"I love you too. You're my forever."

As the sun began to set, the two sat hand in hand with their feet in the Arizona dirt watching the colors in the sky change from yellows and oranges to pinks, purples, and reds.

TURN THE PAGE FOR A SNEAK PEEK AT
SAINT

SAINT

The slam of his office door shook the dust from the old paintings still clinging to the walls of plaster, and the sound of breaking glass confirmed one had lost its battle to hold on. Saint threw yet another folder into his recycling bin before leaning back into his chair and looking up at the stained ceiling. Was he asking too much?

"You send another one packing, boss?" Larry asked as he stuck his head in through the now opened door.

"There has to be one contractor out there who sees my vision for this dump," Saint groaned. "They want to gut everything."

Larry walked all the way in and sat on one of the high-back, upholstered chairs from the lounge area. Saint didn't even know the guy's last name, but that hadn't mattered when he'd found Larry sleeping in the corner of his building's entryway. Larry had needed help and so had Saint. It worked out for both of them. At first, Saint had kept an eye on the young homeless man as he helped around the building, but after two months, Saint had learned to relax a bit. If Larry had intended to steal from him, he would have done it by now.

Saint looked down at his leather-covered hands. The black, fingerless gloves were designed to support and protect his still-healing hands from the wounds that had changed everything. Larry had been indispensable, so Saint had provided him with a room of his own in the back of the building as well as a cash allowance of sorts. Considering Saint paid for all the expenses and food, Larry was pocketing enough to take care of himself without resorting to other means.

"They can't gut what makes this old building unique. My grandpa used to say there was too much conformity in the world," Larry answered as he wiped his sweaty, dust-covered face, leaving one clean streak down the side. Saint wasn't sure where Larry had been raised, but his accent suggested the mid-west.

"Damn straight," Saint agreed before standing with a soft hiss of pain.

"Your side hurting again?" Larry asked.

There had been three bullets that day. One for each hand and a third through his stomach, tearing a hole in his small intestines that had required over ten hours of surgery to repair.

"It's not bad." Short and to the point, Saint refused to talk about his injuries. The quicker he healed, the faster he could put that chapter in his life to rest once and for all.

Larry followed him out of the office Saint had created from the old storage room behind the solid oak bar. He had been surprised no one had ripped it out considering it looked like it dated back to the building's beginnings. The wood was carved into various palm leaf shapes and covered an entire wall complete with mirrors. There was no way in hell he'd allow someone to destroy it, which was one of the many stupid things the last contractor had suggested.

Saint had to hand it to Larry—the man worked hard. "This room looks so much better without all the debris and broken furniture. Were you able to find room in the dumpster out back?"

"Yep, it's all ready for pickup. No wasted space."

"Good job. Are you getting hungry?" Saint asked as he looked down at his watch and discovered it was already early evening. Another day gone and nothing to show for it. Why was finding a general contractor such a pain in the ass? It wasn't as if he was asking for the Taj Mahal to be rebuilt.

"I can keep going, boss."

"That's not what I asked."

Larry looked down at his shoes before mumbling, "I could eat."

Saint knew the young man was doing everything in his power not to be a bother. Sometimes it seemed as though Larry would make himself as small as possible to avoid attention. Saint had been working on the young man's confidence, which seemed ironic considering he'd lost his own.

"You need to tell me the truth when I ask you questions. It's the only way this arrangement is going to work. If I lose track of time, you are free to tell me it's past supper and that you're hungry. At least until we can work a small kitchen in here somewhere so you can make whatever you want whenever. Take a shower and we'll figure out something to eat," Saint instructed, bringing a smile to Larry's face before he took off to his room.

Saint had thought to add more to the common space when they'd cleared out the back, or hub, as they began calling it. Their efforts had yielded a space that included a television, couch, his easy chair, a small dining table set, a coffee table, microwave, electric coffeepot, and a small bar fridge.

Looking around, he wished he had more to show for two months' worth of work, but it wasn't as if he had much else to do. Sure, he could have stayed in a comfortable hotel while working out the basics of his design concept, but if he was starting a new life, he needed to jump in with both feet.

The buzzer for the front door sounded—another new addition— and Saint changed direction and headed toward the thick wooden doors. He'd hired the Sentinel crew to install a security system in the building. It was worth the small fortune he'd paid for the peace of mind. While a lot of DTLA had been or was in the process of being renovated, there were as many places that were derelict and some were hard-core dangerous. Saint had vowed never to be caught unaware again.

He looked at the monitor embedded into the wall a few feet from the front doors, checking to see who was out there. He flipped the locks and walked out into the waning sunlight. The warm air hit him and he shook his head. He didn't think he'd ever get used to LA's climate. Early spring back in New York City would hold the possibility of one last grand snowstorm or two, typically after everyone had removed their snow tires, making traffic worse than usual.

Saint walked the ten feet to the imposing gothic wrought-iron gate that enclosed the front vestibule area of the building. He'd had the gates fixed the day after he'd found Larry sleeping in the entryway. A courier was waiting for him, but instead of opening the nine-foot gate, he simply held out his hand for the man to place the envelope in it.

"Dr. Francis Jeffrey?" The busy street noise and mass of people moving along the sidewalks was almost deafening, and Saint quirked a brow at the kid. He asked the question again and Saint nodded. He was no longer a surgeon and wanted people to address him as mister, but this kid wouldn't know that.

The kid handed a handheld device through the gate's bars. "Sign here," he said in a bored monotone voice. Saint hated this part. Carefully, he took the stylus from the courier and wrapped his fingers as far as he could around the plastic. No matter how hard he tried, he could only make his index finger reach his thumb and scribbled something illegible on the digital pad. When he went to hand back the device, the expression on the kid's face wasn't surprising. Saint growled and shoved the pad in the guy's hands, took the white envelope, and stormed inside before relocking the door.

He wondered if one day it would get better when he saw the shock and pity in their eyes. If the stabbing pain ripping through his heart would ease over time.

"You should have let me get that for you, boss," Larry said as he came running to the front doors. His hair was still damp but at least he was dressed. All Saint needed was a twenty-something traipsing around in a towel.

He treated Larry as he would his brother Johnny, and made that clear after the one and only time the man had made a pass at him. Saint knew it had to have been tough on the street, and Larry probably assumed there would be a price for Saint's kindness. It took some reinforcing, but it seemed Larry believed Saint wanted nothing more than an honest day's work for Larry's efforts. The fact that he felt responsible for Larry and treated him like Johnny, the brother he'd protected by staying away, was a matter Saint didn't want to look at too closely.

ABOUT THE AUTHOR

M. Tasia lives in a small town in Ontario, Canada. She's a member of the Romance Writers of America, and its Rainbow Romance Writers and Toronto Romance Writers chapters. Michelle is a dedicated people-watcher, lover of romance novels, '80s rock, and happy endings. Also, she's the mother of two wonderful girls, wife to a great husband, and a new grandmother, as well as servant to two spoiled furry children who don't seem to realize that they're actually cats.

Michelle writes contemporary and paranormal romance, and she believes love should be celebrated. After all, everybody needs a little romance, excitement, intrigue, and passion in their lives.

Connect with Michelle:
mtasiabooks.com
facebook.com/mtasiabooks
twitter.com/mtasiaauthor
instagram.com/m.tasia.author/

131

www.BOROUGHSPUBLISHINGGROUP.com

If you enjoyed this book, please write a review. Our authors appreciate the feedback, and it helps future readers find books they love. We welcome your comments and invite you to send them to info@boroughspublishinggroup.com. Follow us on Facebook, Twitter and Instagram, and be sure to sign up for our newsletter for surprises and new releases from your favorite authors.

Are you an aspiring writer? Check out www.boroughspublishinggroup.com/submit and see if we can help you make your dreams come true.

www.ingramcontent.com/pod-product-compliance
Lightning Source LLC
Chambersburg PA
CBHW071318130626
46556CB00004B/1652